DYING STAR

BOOK THREE: DARKNESS

SAMSUN LOBE

New Generation Publishing

For Evelyn

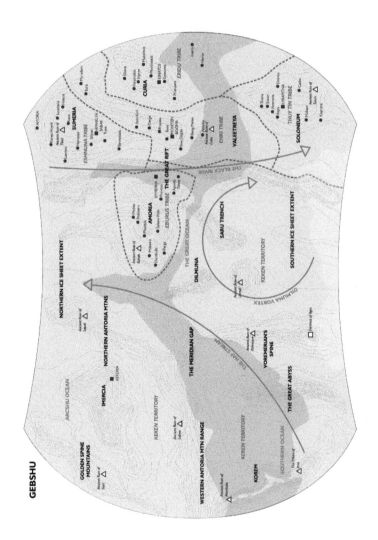

GEBSHU

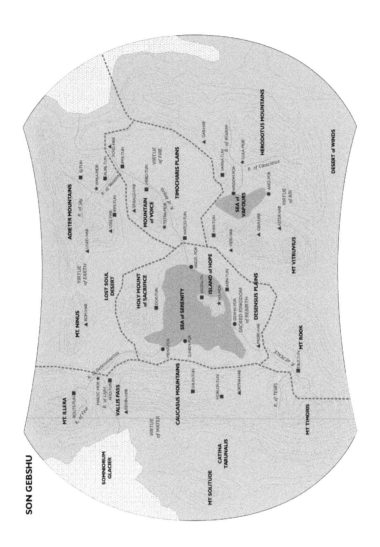

SON GEBSHU

DUMONII

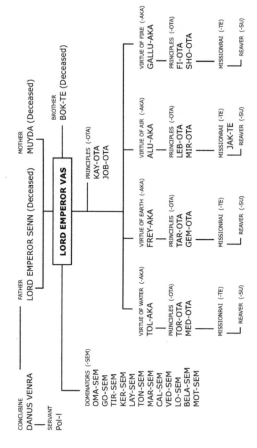

CONCUBINE
DANUS VENRA ———— FATHER
LORD EMPEROR SENN (Deceased)

MOTHER
MUYDA (Deceased)

SERVANT
Pol-I

BROTHER
BOK-TE (Deceased)

LORD EMPEROR VAS

DOMINATORS (-SEM)
OMA-SEM
GO-SEM
TIR-SEM
KER-SEM
LAY-SEM
TON-SEM
MAR-SEM
CAL-SEM
VED-SEM
LO-SEM
BELA-SEM
MOT-SEM

VIRTUE OF WATER (-AKA)
TOL-AKA

PRINCIPLES (-OTA)
TOR-OTA
MED-OTA

MISSIONRAI (-TE)
└ REAVER (-SU)

VIRTUE OF EARTH (-AKA)
FREY-AKA

PRINCIPLES (-OTA)
TAR-OTA
GEM-OTA

MISSIONRAI (-TE)
└ REAVER (-SU)

PRINCIPLES (-OTA)
KAY-OTA
JOB-OTA

VIRTUE OF AIR (-AKA)
ALU-AKA

PRINCIPLES (-OTA)
LEB-OTA
MIR-OTA

MISSIONRAI (-TE)
└ JAK-TE
REAVER (-SU)

VIRTUE OF FIRE (-AKA)
GALLU-AKA

PRINCIPLES (-OTA)
FI-OTA
SHO-OTA

MISSIONRAI (-TE)
└ REAVER (-SU)

Named Women have the prefix 'DANUS'
General population have the suffix '-I'
Special roles within the general population are:
REPLICATOR; MEDICATOR; SERVITOR

OCEAN TRIBES (Enki)

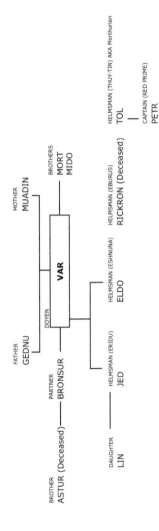

MOTHER
MUADIN

FATHER
GEDNU

BROTHERS
MORT
MIDO

DOYEN

VAR

BROTHER
ASTUR (Deceased)

PARTNER
BRONSUR

HELMSMAN (ESHNUNA)
ELDO

HELMSMAN (EBURUS)
RICKRON (Deceased)

HELMSMAN (THUY-TIN) AKA Merthurian
TOL

CAPTAIN (RED PRIME)
PETR

DAUGHTER
LIN

HELMSMAN (ERIDU)
JED

FORMAL NAMES
Males have the suffix 'son' followed by father's name followed by tribe   eg Var-son-gednu-bay-enki
Females have the suffix 'aon' followed by father's name followed by tribe eg Bronsur-aon-vieto-bay-enki

THE MAGTA

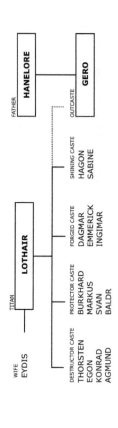

FATHER
HANELORE

OUTCASTE
GERO

TITAN
LOTHAIR

WIFE
EYDIS

DESTRUCTOR CASTE
THORSTEN
EGON
KONRAD
AGMUND

PROTECTOR CASTE
BURKHARD
MARKUS
SVAN
BALDR

FORGED CASTE
DAGMAR
EMMERICK
INGIMAR

SHINING CASTE
HAGON
SABINE

THE SHU SYSTEM

SON TONSHU

LETSHU
Gaseous planet

MI-SON TONSHU

TONSHU
Gas Giant with two moons

RIDDSHU
Dead Planet, was inhabited
before the Star started to die

SON GEBSHU

GEBSHU
Ocean planet with
orbiting moon

ARCSHU
Closet Planet

SHU
Black Dwarf
In final stages of decay

NOT TO SCALE

Book 3 - Darkness

Prologue

All things end. Some things end in a heartbeat and other things take so long that they can appear immortal. However long the journey the inevitable darkness will always be there to claim its final embrace.

The last people of the ocean world Gebshu struggle to comprehend the death of their star and their planet. The minute decay over thousands of millennia has been so slow it has gone unnoticed. Now when life starts to fade with every rise and fall of the moon, they start to fear.

There are those that can see the approaching darkness and cling to the slightest hope, renewing vows to long forgotten Gods. There are those prepared to embrace the end, comfortable they have fulfilled the purpose of their existence, resigned to their fate. Then there are those who are blind to even the brightest signals of the apocalypse, unbelieving and unwavering in their stubbornness to survive.

All of these people, regardless of their origins and their view on the end of all consciousness, have the primal need for something greater than themselves. Perhaps this is a father, a creator, a watcher or simply a friend. In the end they are all the same eternal being. This singular need has the ability to overwhelm rational thought and logic. Can such a being, borne from emotion, truly have the power to change the future?

Can this God coax a dying star back to life? Can this God save his people from extinction? Can this God defy the inevitable? Can this God bring light to the darkness?

Whether he can or cannot it is the glimmer of hope that he provides that keeps him alive in the minds of men. It is hope that the people of Gebshu now nurture like their first born. But even hope has to end. All things end.

Chapter 01 - Betrayal

The dying star had already set yet the crisp white surface of snow still reflected enough light for Var to make out the familiar details of his home. The fortress city of Asturia was a welcome and comforting sight. The many moons spent travelling from the deep South had given him time to think and reflect. His melancholy mood quickly evaporated as he eyes followed the outline of the spire crowning the cathedral.

A few more of the living pods had appeared. Each linked to another via rope bridges and pulley systems, like arteries connecting vital organs. Apart from that everything looked as it had half a season ago, at least from the outside.

Var slowed his pace as he reached the outer harbour wall. He flattened himself against the massive stonework, panting hard, the cold air stinging his lungs.

"You're out of shape" came the matter of fact comment from the gloom. The Emperor padded to a stop next to the breathless Helmsman. Var looked up into his shadowed features. Even in the low light he could see the lack of exertion on his face. A serine smile crept across his regal features.

"Well I made it here first" suggested Var.

"True enough" said the Emperor. "But we were following you, remember?" Var grunted regaining his composure as the last of the Emperor's Dominators loped in, all equally nonplussed by the vast distance they had just covered.

They had left the ice yachts some way from the island of Imercia. They had been cautious in their approach not knowing what waited for them at the tribesman's former home. The Magta and the remnants of the Emperor's army had stayed behind. Under Lothair's and Tol-Aka's supervision they were making their way to the ancient ruins of Labna. There they would prepare for the second part of the plan.

Var led the men around the edge of the outer harbour wall to where it met the earlier building phase. Two round towers marked the old entrance to the sea port, long since redundant as the ocean had retreated. All of the harbour now seemed pointless as it was held in the vice-like grip of the pack ice.

Var spotted the jutting stones he had been searching for and quickly started to climb the wall. The snow on the small handholds stung his fingers as he hauled his weight upwards. He peered over the top. There were footprints in the snow all along the wall walk, but there was no sign of movement.

One by one the group crested the wall. They made their way as silently as they could through the ramshackle buildings that occupied the majority of surface area atop the huge harbour walls. The occasional crunch of snow underfoot was drowned out by the noise coming from within the wooden shelters. The occasional child's cry mixed with cacophony of domestic chores.

As they approached the inner gate, Var raised his hand signalling 'Halt'. The group crouched and each individual did their best to blend into the environment.

"What do you see?" asked the Emperor.

"A guard. I am not sure if it's one of my men." Var took out his small monocular and placed the cold metal bezel against his eye socket. The guard was dressed as they all were, head to toe in furs and skins. He watched as the man huffed into his mitted hands before clapping them together. He moved to one edge and briefly turned to look out to sea, before turning to disappear out of sight once more. In that instant Var had seen all that he needed. A red stripe running down the guards face. Starting above his eye and finishing on his lower jaw. Var turned to the Emperor.

"We need the Nightsigh."

Without a word the Emperor turned to his men and clicked his fingers. The Dominator Mar-Sem had been entrusted with the unique Magta weapon. He shuffled forward as the Emperor pointed towards the tower.

"Do I wait until I can see him?" he whispered.

"You don't have to see your target" answered Var.

"Just get the arrow through the opening. It will do the rest."

Mar-Sem nodded his understanding and respectfully removed the ornate long-bow from its cover. Placing the bow between his legs he bent the limbs as he had been shown in order to string it.

"Are you sure there is just one of them?" asked the Emperor.

"We'll soon find out" smiled Var.

Mar-Sem screwed the heavy arrow tip onto the shaft and notched it across the bow. He moved cautiously from his hiding place and into a small clearing between the houses. He arched his back, battling to draw back the bow. He brought the string to his pursed lips. Despite his considerable strength he was struggling with the weapon that was designed for the giant Magta. Sure of his aim he loosed the arrow. The string sang a delicate tune as the projectile sped towards the tower. The arrow sailed through the small turret opening and disappeared.

Mar-Sem crouched back down next to the others, all of them waiting apprehensively, expecting any moment for the alarm to be raised.

"How does it work?" asked the Dominator.

"I'm not sure exactly" replied Var. "It's something to do with sound. The arrow head can home in on a heartbeat, or something like that."

They waited for several moments without the re-appearance of the guard or the alarm sounding, so decided it was safe to move. As they crept up the steps to the inner fortress they split up as planned and vanished inside the city buildings.

Even though Var knew every inch of the city, where every hidden alcove was, where the guards were likely to congregate, he felt uncomfortable in the presence of the Emperor and his Dominators. He watched them confidently stride off, no hint of fear or doubt. They had been born for this, trained all their lives for combat and martial prowess. He had no misgivings about their abilities; they would complete their missions. His worry was that he would fail them. He shook his head trying to dislodge his concerns.

He headed into the labyrinth of corridors heading towards the kitchen. When he had lived here the long hallway outside of the kitchen was a common place for the guards to meet. The warmth and smell tempting them away from their duties. They had not been sure there would be any Merthurian guards in the city at all. As it was, it looked they had left just a handful. They obviously felt no threat from the people of Asturia. Var was sure Bronsur had a major part to play in that situation.

Var crept into the hallway, his target ahead of him. The guard was bent over fiddling with the buckles on his greaves. Var tried to move silently keeping the weight on his toes. This was proving difficult with his sprung artificial limb.

As he closed in on the warrior he inadvertently dragged his boot and the Merthurian guard span in surprise. Before the guard could draw his weapon Var thundered a sweeping kick towards his knee. The disadvantage of the prosthetic limb was now lost as the metal and wood of Var's lower leg cracked against the guard's knee. The weight and momentum swept the soldier's leg away sending him flailing onto the floor.

Var pressed his advantage leaping onto the prone soldier, but as he did the guard lashed upwards. His fist missed but the following elbow slammed into Var's chin. His head felt heavy and his vision started to cloud. His opponent wasted no time and turned his body weight throwing Var onto the cold stone walkway. The Red Prime guard was no stranger to combat and recovering from the initial shock attack now rained down punch after punch trying to knock out his assailant. Var's natural instincts took over, bringing his arms up to shield himself from the onslaught. He reached up grabbing the guards armour and dragged him close to his chest so that he couldn't get the leverage for further blows.

Holding the guard, Var tried to roll. He succeeded in moving onto his front, but the warrior stayed with him slipping his forearm under Var's chin and clasping his arm with his other hand. He started to squeeze. Var could feel his consciousness fleeing and desperately tried to pry the guard's fingers free.

The soldier grunted and Var breathed in relief as his attacker's grip faded. Var felt the sudden dead weight of the man and the warm trickle of blood on the back of his neck. He rolled, throwing the limp body to one side, kicking to free his legs.

Standing in the hallway, blood dripping from his knife, was the Emperor.

"I had it covered" suggested Var.

"Of course" came the reply.

Var puffed out his chest trying to conjure up his lost pride. The torch light bounced off the Emperor's features and he saw no sign of malice or contempt. If it had been Gero he wouldn't have heard the last of it. The Emperor's outlook was simply matter of fact. The task at hand was complete and that was enough.

The two men continued through the hallway and silently crept up a small spiral staircase leading to the main keep. The small archway at the top of the stairwell opened onto a main walkway. From here numerous doors led off into private chambers and the main staircase fanned upwards towards the great hall.

Noise erupted from their right and they ducked back down into the darkness in unison. A young woman carrying empty pots and pans rounded the corner. She turned into the archway and attempted to make her way down the stairs to the kitchen. As she saw the two figures crouching in the shadows she dropped the pans and was about to scream. Var clamped his hand firmly over her mouth and looked into her eyes.

"It's me, the Doyen, please do not scream" he whispered. Recognition and then understanding flashed across her eyes and Var gently released his grip. He had managed to stop her screaming but the clatter of pots and pans on the stonework would surely bring unwanted attention.

"You're back!" exclaimed the woman. "I must..."

"Please keep your voice down" interrupted Var. "No-one must know we are here."

They heard a latch lift and drop and the creak of door hinges out in the corridor. Var put his finger over his lips and moved back down into the stairwell. The young woman acting startled turned to see one of the Red Prime guards smiling jovially and walking towards her.

"Are you alright? I am sorry I didn't mean to alarm you" said the guard.

"Yes of course" replied the woman organising her thoughts. "I'm so clumsy, I tripped and dropped everything."

"Here let me give you a hand" offered the guard.

"No, No it's quite alright. Thank you for your offer of help." She quickly picked up the utensils and made her way down the stairs. The guard lazily took one last look around and headed back towards the open door. As the shaking woman passed Var he mouthed the words 'Thank You'. She smiled back, but the smile quickly faded as she locked eyes with the Emperor. The huge frame of Lord Vas nudged Var to one side and sped down the hallway his knife drawn. He grabbed the guard by the hair ripping his head back and plunging his knife into the man's throat. He tore it out to the side severing the jugular and windpipe. He withdrew the blade and then rammed it into the back of the dead man's skull.

As he did a second guard rounded the corner behind him. Before he could shout, Var jumped from the stairwell and lunged forward with his sword. The razor sharp Magta blade passed straight through the surprised guard's stomach plate, through his abdomen and severed his spinal cord. He span withdrawing his sword at the same time, looking back towards the Emperor. The tall warrior strode up the hallway and past Var without so much as a look of recognition.

"You're welcome" said Var with as much sarcasm as he could muster. He watched as the Emperor placed his armoured boot on the chest of the fallen soldier and curled his fingers around the hilt of his knife. The blade was firmly lodged in the eye socket of the Red Prime soldier. He tore it free and the ruined eyeball came with it. He wiped the popped eye sack on the dead man's jerkin. He gestured to Var pointing down the hallway.

"Shall we continue?" he suggested.

*

On the far side of the city was the postern gate. When Var had last been here this was used as the main point of access to the sea pods. These were the living accommodation of all of the sea tribes that had migrated to Asturia when the oceans started to freeze. Since the Red Prime's peaceful occupation it had been used as the main gateway to the encamped forces of the Merthurian army. It was the nearest entrance to the huge force, and had recently been in constant use.

The three Dominators that had been assigned to secure the gate crept silently along the battlements of the curtain wall. As they reached the end, they tried the small wooden door to the tower. It was locked. Below them under the portcullis were five guards that they could see. The noise from the lower barracks told them that there were more inside.

Ton-Sem signalled upwards to his brothers as they had all heard a guard in the lookout tower above cough loudly. Ton-Sem put his back to the door and linked his fingers together forming a foothold. Go-Sem placed his boot on the makeshift step and hauled himself upwards. He carefully searched the stonework for handholds before he climbed again so that he was standing on Ton-Sem's shoulders. As careful as he was his metal breastplate clacked against the stone. Go-Sem looked up. A red faced guard peered over the edge of the tower. Without hesitation Go-Sem flexed his legs and launched himself up into the air, reaching out for the stunned guard. His mailed fists clamped tightly to the guards fur jacket and as he fell back to the walkway he dragged the helpless soldier with him.

As he landed he used his own momentum to aid gravity by pulling the screaming soldier head first into the stone slabs. Ton-Sem winced at the sound of bone crunching and the unnatural angle of the dead look-out's neck.

"So much for stealth" muttered Cal-Sem unsheathing his bolt gun. Rubbing his calf muscles, Go-Sem turned to scowl at his brother in arms.

"That thing won't work here" he grunted. He pointed towards Cal-Sem's un-holstered gun. "They didn't work properly back home on the moon, you'll have no chance here. The mechanism freezes solid."

Undeterred Cal-Sem smashed the weapon against the parapet, urging it to work, if for nothing else but to prove his comrade wrong. As predicted, nothing happened. He looked over the side of the wall at the Red Prime guards scurrying around trying to work out from where the noise had emanated. He threw the useless bolt gun at the nearest guard and swiftly followed behind it.

The gun bounced harmlessly off the guard's shoulder, but the follow up thrust from Cal-Sem's blade shattered his teeth as the Dominator rammed his sword through the shocked soldier's mouth. The dead weight of the warrior turned the hilt in Cal-Sem's hand as he fell. He quickly realised that in his eagerness for the kill the sword point was stuck firmly in the dead man's skull.

Four more Red Prime ran from the guardhouse to join forces, whilst another sprinted down the steep slope away from the gate.

"Ton! One of them is trying to raise the alarm" shouted Cal-Sem.

"Already on it" replied the Dominator.

As Cal-Sem drew two curved knives, Go-Sem dropped down beside him.

"Lost your sword already" he laughed.

"Thought I would give them a chance" he shrugged.

Go-Sem unpinned two shiva that were strapped to his back. They were a traditional weapon of the Dumonii. They consisted of a crescent blade under which a grab handle was fixed. The weapon was used to punch and swipe and was a favourite weapon of the Dominators. It was particularly effective in close combat.

Their adversaries advanced quickly trying to use their

weight in numbers to overcome the two Dominators.

Cal-Sem side stepped the attack thundering a low kick at the oncoming guard. It was blocked but gave him enough time to shoulder charge another of the soldiers. The force bloodied the man's mouth and sent him skidding into the snow. He raised both knives to block an overhead sword swing. Before he could step back the point of a Red Prime's sword dug into his midriff. Grabbing the blade Cal-Sem stepped back dragging the warrior forward. As he stumbled towards the Dominator, Cal-Sem lurched forward stabbing the blade up under the soldier's chest plate piercing his heart. He flipped the newly acquired sword over catching it by the hilt, just in time to parry the next thrust.

Go-Sem was more cautious. He moved with purpose, eyeing his enemies, looking for an opening. One of the Red Prime swung his mace wildly trying to force the encounter. The warrior to his left followed in behind the swing lunging for the Dominator's thigh with his sword. Go-Sem stepped back, calmly parried the blow with his left shiva and then hammered his right blade into the exposed side of the attacker's head. The crescent blade bit deeply into the brain pan. Screaming with pain the man fell to his knees, holding his head.

Now the Dominator attacked. He jumped forward launching an upper cut that cleanly sheared through the jaw of the nearest Red Prime soldier. He then pirouetted in the air slicing down across another guard. The helmet took the brunt of the attack with the blade just nicking the guard's cheek. The guard had no time to dwell on his luck, as Go-Sem who seemed continually in motion spiralled around again bringing his second shiva to bear. This time the blade sliced through the chinstrap, through his lower ear and across his throat. Dark blood bubbled up from the wound and from his mouth. As he dropped, Go-Sem's knee struck hard into the downed man's face sending him flying back, blood spraying skyward.

"Four down, four to go" smiled Cal-Sem.

"Are you sure you can keep up" replied Go-Sem. "You seem to have misplaced some of your blood." He gestured towards the red stain on Cal-Sem's side. The Dominator touched the wound and smiled.

"I have too much blood as it is. It was just slowing me down."

With four of their number either dead or incapacitated most soldiers would have turned and ran. These weren't most soldiers. They were Red Prime. They were handpicked from the hordes of the Merthurian army. Singled out for their skill and devotion in battle. The two vertical red streaks across their faces was a sign of their elite rank.

They focussed on the pair in front of them and without words all knew the plan of action. Separate, them, then focus on the injured one. Three of them were armed with traditional sabres and shields whilst the other held a long halberd. The pole-arm was normally used when mounted. It had a curved blade with a reverse hook on the back and a spear point at the other end. He lowered the weapon and advanced.

The injured man suddenly leapt towards them, his stolen sword clattering against a raised shield boss. The shield had blocked the strike but did not stop the knife blade which followed. The slender blade drove upwards piercing the guard's bicep. Gritting his teeth against the pain the Red Prime soldier swung his shield smashing it into the face of his attacker. He followed with a sword jab which was deflected before he swung his shield again, this time catching him square in the face and knocking him to the ground.

The three men surrounded the downed Dominator, whilst the other was desperately trying to keep his friend from coming to his aid.

"You hit like a woman" spat Cal-Sem standing slowly. The sword in his left arm felt heavy in his grip. Heavier than it should. He knew he was losing too much blood. He ran and jumped. The injured Red Prime soldier lifted his shield as expected and rather than striking the Dominator used the shield to catapult himself over the warrior and land behind him. He swung his sword in a wide arc before turning on the soldier he had just vaulted. This time Cal-Sem jabbed his knife into the man's ear killing him instantly. He didn't have time to turn and felt the warm numb pain from repeated sword strikes in his back. He smiled peacefully as the white blanket of ground came towards him.

Go-Sem looked on despairingly. The guard was doing a good job keeping him at weapon's length. Without engaging him it was a stalemate. He saw Cal-Sem fall and his rising anger gave him an involuntary snarl .

He feigned a surge forward. The soldier took the bait and lurched out with the long weapon. Go-Sem batted the blade down and then stamped hard on the wooden haft. The shaft splintered. Moving forward the Dominator deflected a feeble strike with broken pole-arm before punching down with his shiva. The blade severed the guard's hand at the wrist. With a disdainful swing he severed the screaming man's throat before dropping to one knee and punching up beneath the plate mail skirt.

"Which one of you two wants a gender change first" sneered Go-Sem. The nearest guard attacked, swinging first low and then high in a flurry of attacks. The Dominator expertly blocked the strikes, but equally none of his returns were getting through either, each skimming harmlessly off the shield.

Go-Sem stamped forward pinning the soldier's foot. He blocked a sword swipe before dropping to the ground and punching where his foot had been. The sharp blade of the shiva severed the guard's toes and sliced into the frozen ground.

Go-Sem expected the pain of the wound to slow the man

down. Instead the soldier pushed forward on his ruined foot stabbing downwards with his sword. The curved blade parted the straps on his shoulder plate and the blade sank deep into his flesh. Ignoring the white hot pain he punched up half chopping through the arm that had him pinned. He punched up again sinking his other blade deep into the guard's upper thigh.

Thinking of the remaining soldier he stood to witness the long chain of Ton-Sem's kuri wrap around the guard's throat. Safe in the knowledge their mission was successful he stood straddling the prone guard. He pulled the blade out of his shoulder and threw it to one side. The Red Prime was fearfully trying to back away from the stalking Dominator. Blood was pouring from his arm and his ruptured femoral artery. Go-Sem kicked the shield away and dropped down onto his knees pinning the guard's torso.

"For my brother" he snorted.

It was not until he felt Ton-Sem's hand on his shoulder that the big Dominator stopped punching. The bloodlust withdrew and his vision returned. Warm blood dripped off his chin and he felt the sticky liquid squelch in both his hands. There was nothing left of the soldier's upper body except chunks of flesh, bone and ruptured organs.

"Come brother" said Ton-Sem. "We must inform the Emperor."

*

Var and the Emperor made their way to the top of the keep without any further encounters. As they approached Bronsur's room they heard laughter from within. Var's heart was pounding in his chest. He was desperate to see his betrothed after his long absence, but he felt a niggling pang of doubt. The deep rumble of male laughter was only adding to it. He grabbed the handle about to walk in, but then hesitated. He stepped back and knocked on the door.

The door opened slowly and Bronsur still in conversation with her guest turned her head. She stopped as if frozen in the ice along with her city. A beaming smile suddenly melted across her face and with tears welling in her eyes she threw her arms around Var's neck. He stood unmoving, lost in the moment, not wanting to speak or move, less it would end the warm feeling that now caressed his soul.

Movement elsewhere in the room shattered his peace and he looked over Bronsur's shoulder to see a tall Red Prime guard get up from his old wooden rocking chair. The man smiled and moved towards him.

"I do not believe we have...." The guard's cordial introduction was cut short. Before Var could even get a word out the Emperor had moved past him his war hammer extending in his hand. He drove the still unfolding metal head into the guard's temple. The blow fractured the skull killing him instantly. His dead body bounced comically from the end of the bed before collapsing onto the wooden floor. Both Bronsur and Var stood wide mouthed.

"What is going on? What have you done? Var?" came the flurry of questions from Bronsur as she knelt at the dead man's side. "Who in the name of the Gods is this monster?" She pointed an accusing finger at the Emperor.

"I'll rendezvous with the rest of my men. Come and find me when you have sorted this situation" said the Emperor. Without any further ceremony he turned and strode from the room.

"It's a long story" Var started. "Those men, you have no idea what they are like."

"Really?" interrupted Bronsur. "This man was my friend. His name was Jerard. He and his men have been staying at the castle as our guests. How dare you and that idiot just burst in here." Emotion welled up inside her and she placed her hand gently on the dead guard's forehead.

"Just how friendly were you?" asked Var. Bronsur glared up at him and in that moment he knew the answer, and knew also he should have not asked the question. "I'm sorry" he pleaded.

"I think it's time you explained it all to me" suggested Bronsur. Var sighed deeply and moved to hold Bronsur's hand. She drew away sharply.

"Whoever you think this man is, and whether or not he has been a peaceful guest here, you do not know what they are capable of. They are called the Red Prime, but they are part of a much bigger army known as the Merthurian."

"Do you think me stupid?" demanded Bronsur. Var shrugged his shoulders, unsure of why she was asking the question. "I know exactly who this man is. Yes he is, was, a sergeant in the Red Prime. He and his Captain, Petr, have been visiting the castle since they arrived over twenty moons ago. I know they are professional soldiers, that is why I accepted their offer to patrol the city. I also know there is a large force camped out on the ice less than an arrow's distance from our walls. They have been courteous and helpful. What did you expect me to do? The ocean tribes have no interest in conflict, especially one in which we would lose. " She stood and looked down at the prone figure.

"And now this. They will not stand by once they find out."

"They have no intention of standing by" snapped Var. "I have seen the destruction they bring. They have all but wiped the Magta from this world. They have no intention of stopping until all of the people of this planet are either dead or subjugated. We came here to fetch our people and move before they have a chance to stop us."

"The Magta? Gero and Hanelore's race? What happened?" asked Bronsur.

"The Red Prime are just a small part of this army.

They are led by a Helmsman called Toll-Son-Ray. He besieged the Magta's home, and apart from the scarce few that escaped with me they were all slaughtered. Women and children Bron, they don't care."

"They have not mentioned any Helmsman. I thought Petr to be in charge."

"I wonder why that could be?" said Var sarcastically. He could see his words were gradually taking hold in her mind.

"But the Magta. You met with them seasons ago, asking for help. They refused, and that was to help one of their own."

"That's true" conceded Var. "Gero has a special talent for annoying those close to him. It's a complicated story, but the leader of the Magta - Lothair, is Gero's brother. As well as that, Hanelore is their father. I believe it had something to do with a woman."

Bronsur raised her eyebrows. Strangely the thought of the Magta involved in romantic trysts had not crossed her mind before.

"Where are they now?" asked Bronsur.

"We could not risk the Merthurian seeing them at the city. They are at the ruins of Labna waiting for us."

"And who was that brute that did this?" she questioned.

"He is the Emperor or rather was the Emperor of the Dumonii." Var waited for the explosion of rage.

"And you two are friends?"

"Sort of" replied Var. "We have had our differences, but you know the old saying, the enemy of my enemy and all that. Besides without him, we wouldn't have made it back here - The Merthurian would have overrun us for sure."

Bronsur shook her head, trying to put the disjointed facts she was hearing into some sort of order.

"So what's the plan? Are we leaving Asturia to settle elsewhere, or is this simply to defeat the Red Prime?"

"The Red Prime, although our immediate concern, are simply delaying us. The Kekken have also come back into play. I think they may well also be hostile towards us."

"So basically everyone or everything is out to kill us, and you want to leave this fortress and make a run for it?"

"When you put it like that" Var smiled. "It makes no difference whether we run or stay and fight. There is another purpose. I have the key. It is the key to the gateway to the Gods. That is where we must go. Whether we die at the hands of the Merthurian or the Kekken, remaining here on this world one thing is certain. We will die. The only hope for us, and our people is to reach the Gods, and pray they will listen. I have always known I had a purpose, and this is it"

Bronsur crossed the room and placed her arms once again around his neck.

"You know I don't believe in the Gods and neither do most of our people."

Var was about to defend his destiny, when she placed her delicate finger across his lips.

"I believe in you Var, and so do the people. That is enough." She leaned in and kissed him gently. "I have missed you my love."

*

"I don't like it" stated the Emperor.

"I trust her" replied Var.

"It's not your betrothed that concerns me" said the Emperor.

After emotional reunions with the rest of his family, Var had introduced them to the Emperor and filled them in on the events of the past season, including the demise of the Magta. He patiently explained the plan of the alliance and was surprised at how easily they accepted his explanation.

Bronsur had told them that Petr, the captain of the Red Prime was due to visit that evening. They had carefully constructed a water-tight trap which no warrior, no matter how great, would be able to escape. With Petr and his entourage dead they would begin the evacuation of the city.

Bronsur had urged Var to let her take a welcoming party down to meet the Red Prime captain. Insisting anything less would arouse suspicion. It was this party of Bronsur, Var's mother and father and his twin brothers that Var and the Emperor now watched, as they wound their way down the steep path and out onto the ice.

They could make out a flurry of snow that was being kicked up by the advancing soldiers. As they closed the distance Var's gut knotted as the hulking Shektars came into focus.

*

Mort blew the snow off from his fur collar into the face of his brother.

"Hey!" complained Mido.

"Cut it out you two" demanded Gednu. "Remember nothing should seem out of place. Concentrate for once."

Ignoring his father Mido flicked snow back at his brother.

"I give up" complained Gednu. Muadin hugged his arm trying to placate her betrothed. Bronsur turned to the group.

"Just let me handle things" she admonished.

They stood in renewed silence as they watched the gigantic beasts of the Red Prime lope ever closer. As they neared, Petr's four flanking riders started to dismount, and the Captain pulled down the shemagh from his face.

"It's fresh this evening" said Petr amicably.

"That it is" answered Bronsur.

"There was no need to come out to meet me. I know my way now" smiled the Captain.

"Yes I know" replied Bronsur. Her tone was losing its friendly lilt, a subtlety only picked up by Petr.

"Is there a problem?" he asked. Bronsur cast a nervous glance around to her father in law.

"There is I'm afraid" she replied.

"Bron! What are you doing?" yelled Gednu.

"It's OK Gednu, this is for the best, for all of us" soothed Bronsur   . She moved towards Petr. His Shektar flinched and snorted. She could smell its hot breath as she neared the rider. "I must speak to you plainly" she explained.

Petr twisted in his saddle and lent over towards her.

"We have always spoken that way" said Petr. "What is on your mind?"

"I know why you are here, you and your men. I was hoping to talk to you, to reason with you in order to save further bloodshed" said Bronsur.

"Further bloodshed?" questioned the Captain as he looked up towards the city walls searching for an answer.

"I know you are an honourable man Petr. From the short time we have known each other I know that to be true. I would like to consider us friends. As a friend I would ask a favour of you. Return to your camp and leave us in peace. Death awaits you and your men inside the gates." she explained. Petr looked up at the great city and then keenly eyed Var's family.

"So, you would save my life in exchange for your people?" asked the Captain. "What of the lives of my men inside your fortress. Do they still live? Or do you intend to exchange your lives for theirs" he snarled.

In that briefest of moments she saw deep into the rider's soul and re-coiled with fear at what she had glimpsed.

"What has happened could not be stopped. My betrothed has returned, he only looks to protect his people. I would gladly give my life to put a stop to this madness" she stammered.

"That is not your choice!" he bellowed. He spurred his mount and the giant beast lurched up into the air. Its massive paw batted Bronsur to the ice. The Shektar returned to the ground pinning her beneath its massive paw. Mort and Mido leapt into action, but before they could get close to Bronsur the Red Prime guards were upon them. The pommel of a sword crashed into the back of Mido's head and he plummeted face first unconscious into the snow. Mort received a heavy kick in the stomach and as he doubled over the soldier grabbed his arm forcing it upwards and then forcing him down onto the floor. Gleefully a guard stepped in and launched a thunderous kick at the boy's head. His head jerked backwards and his eyes rolled as he succumbed to the darkness. Gednu stepped forward drawing his sword. He shook off his betrothed's desperate grip.

"You coward!" growled Gednu.

Petr vaulted from his mount in one swift move. The Shektar remaining in place still pinning Bronsur to the frozen ground. He drew his own blade .

"Tell me old man. Bronsur's betrothed. He is your son?" asked Petr.

"He will rip the eyes from your skull, and cast you into the depths" swore Gednu.

"Well make sure you tell him I will do much worse to his woman, and when I finally tire of her attentions I will feed her broken body to my beast." In one swift move Petr's arm flashed forward his sword slicing into Gednu's stomach. The Red Prime Captain stood over Var's father as he thudded to his knees. His screaming betrothed coming between the two men.

Petr ignored her cries and looked to the distance at the group of people running out from the city gates towards them.

"We are taking the woman and the boys with us" commanded Petr. "This fight will keep for another day." He chuckled to himself and he climbed back onto his mount. With one final glance over his shoulder they rode back towards the Merthurian camp.

*

Var's lungs burned and his muscles strained as he tried to chase the fleeing riders. He finally stopped, bending double trying to regain his breath. He felt a hand on his shoulder.

"We will get them back" said the Emperor simply.

Var looked back at the rest of the Dominators who stood around his mother and father. With his remaining reserves of energy he sprinted back to the group. Skidding to a halt he crouched grasping his father's hand. The hand was limp. His mother sobbed uncontrollably. Var looked down at the serene features of his father. He gently closed his unseeing eyes, and burrowed his head into the dead man's chest. Tears rolled down his cheeks.

"I told Bronsur that it didn't matter whether we ran or whether we stayed and fought. That we had a greater purpose in this world. That changes now. I promise you this father, I will not stop until every last

Merthurian embraces the darkness. That is the only purpose left to me now."

Chapter 2 - Last Stand

Petr approached the tent of Tol-Son-Ray dragging his gagged prisoner by the hair. Bronsur squirmed under his grip. Muffled screams and shouts was all she could do to annoy her captor, as both her hands and feet were bound. The Captain tiring of the muted complaints turned, lashing out with a back hand strike. The force knocked Bronsur out cold.

"Have you two fallen out?" came the question from behind Petr.

"It is as I predicted" muttered the Red Prime Captain turning to greet the Helmsman.

"Is there something on your mind Petr? Well? Spit it out man" demanded Tol-Son-Ray.

"I urged you to take the fortress when we first arrived. We have waited for nothing. Our advantage is lost. Her betrothed has returned and with him I assume the remnants of the giant army. This means we will lose men unnecessarily, having to lay siege to another fortress. I know you follow the old hag's visions but this makes no sense."

The leader of the Merthurian stepped forward and knelt down beside the still body of Bronsur. He lifted her head and then let it fall back into the snow.

"You have enjoyed these last few moons in her company my friend. It is natural for you to be aggravated by these events. But please don't presume to lecture me on what is necessary and what is not. The old witch has predicted everything that has come to pass. If she says 'wait', then we wait."

Petr calmed his growing anger. He knew when he could push the Helmsman and now was not one of those times. There had been no news from the force he had sent to chase down the last of the Magta. That meant only one thing. Bad news.

"I will talk with the crone again" added Tol-Son-Ray. "We will see if your eagerness for action is mirrored in her scratchings."

The tall leader made his way through the myriad of tents that made up the encampment. On the outskirts of the camp and separated from the main force by a waist high circular wall of ice was the tent of the Morrg. Most of the ocean tribes had shamans or seers of some description, with purported powers of healing, path reading or other such arcane abilities. The Merthurian's own soothsayer was known as the Morrg. Her origin was unknown, and the methods she used had strayed some distance from the simple homeopathy employed by most of her ilk.

Her tent, like most of the Merthurian abodes was a domed construction made from bone and skins. Snow was then piled over the frame to insulate its occupants from the freezing temperatures outside. It gave them a quick and efficient method for making and breaking camp. Apart from the wall that surrounded her tent the clear difference between the Morrg's home and the rest of the Merthurian was the blood splattered snow and seemingly random animal bones and body parts that littered the ground inside the encampment. Strange glyphs had been carved into the ice and then filled with blood. These dark markings had been fastidiously cleaned of snow and despite the sub zero temperatures the blood strangely remained as a liquid.

Tol spat onto the ground. He trusted the word of the Morrg more than anything, but her methods frightened him. He was ashamed of his fear. Fear of the unknown.

"I'll make you clean that up young Tol" came the rasping voice from within the tent. He breathed deeply and crouched to enter.

The Morrg sat crossed legged on thin animal fur. She was almost naked apart from thin wrappings that covered her chest and hips. She was impossibly old, her pale sallow skin hung on her bones like clothes on a washing line. Her entire skin was covered in crude tattoos. Mysterious writings and symbols that had faded over time, the edges bleeding making them appear more like stains than decoration. Her long white hair hung down her back and seemed so brittle that it might snap at any moment. Her face was that of a skin coloured skull. Her thin lips had retreated away from her mouth showing her black gums and crooked teeth. If it wasn't for her eyes, it would have been easy to mistake her for a corpse.

Her eyes burned. Glowing red orbs that sucked the attention from anyone in her presence like inescapable whirlpools. They pulsed with a ceaseless chaotic beat, unblinking, all seeing.

Tol's eyes narrowed as he sat opposite. He tried and failed to avoid her gaze.

"What's the matter my love? Surely you have not tired of my beauty?" said the Morrg cackling. She opened a small drawstring bag in front of her. In it was a variety of tablets and vials. She removed the cork from a small glass bottle. Guttural sounds emanated from her lipless mouth as a mist quickly filled the confined space.

Tol coughed. The acrid vapour stung his eyes and he brought his hands up to rub them. The green mist quickly evaporated as did the burning sensation. As he opened his eyes he rubbed them once more not believing what they relayed.

The former witch was transformed. Her white hair was now black and it flowed over her lithe naked shoulders. Her body was now that of a nubile young woman. The flimsy rags now strained to contain her ample breast. Her face was that of symmetrical perfection, dark tempting brown eyes and full red lips. She smiled revealing an ivory white row of flawless teeth.

"Is this more to your liking my love?" Her silky smooth voice enchanting his mind. "Surely you recognise me?" she continued, tilting her head to one side. Recognition flashed across Tol-Son-Ray's face as the memory of the succubus flooded back, unwelcome into his thoughts. He urged as the truth of his past conquest became clear. He could not control the bile rising in his throat and vomited onto the floor. The moment the hot liquid hit the ice the glamour ceased. The old hag now sat before him once more. He emptied the contents of his stomach again.

"Charming" croaked the Morrg. "But necessary nonetheless. Do not worry my love. Most of the men in your charge have enjoyed my embrace in one form or another. "

Still recovering from the revelation, Tol-Son-Ray watched as she tossed several of the bone tablets into the pool of sick. With her long cracked fingernails she mixed them together. She opened another small bottle and the pungent smell instantly kicked the senses of the Merthurian leader. She poured the sticky fluid onto the ground. A flame erupted from the ground and as the smoke and fire dissipated only the bone tablets were left on the discoloured floor. The Morrg reached out and grabbed Tol's hands.

"Don't worry my love. All is as I promised."

"I just came to get..."

"I know why you are here" interrupted the old woman. "You fear things are slipping from your grasp; that maybe that whelp of a captain is right, that you have waited too long. You seek my re-assurance." She stroked his hand with her long calloused fingers. "The time is fast approaching. You will have your victory. The world you seek to rule will be yours. Nothing will be able to withstand your forces. Your mighty army will swallow everything in its path. My vision has not changed from the first time you came to my counsel. I still see you sat on a throne, your enemies crushed at your feet. You will rule unchallenged until the day I call to you from the depths. " The Morrg stared down at the floor once more. "The frightened prey of the nearby citadel will run for their lives and you will hunt them down. As our star rises on the morrow gather your forces and claim your destiny my love."

The Morrg withdrew her hands and her bright eyes slowly dimmed as she faded into a lifeless trance. Tol removed himself from the tent as quickly as he could. The cold air washed over him like a cleansing shower. As he strode out of the witch's circle he noticed Petr waiting for him.

"Tomorrow morning" he muttered as he hurried past his captain.

*

The Merthurian camp bristled with action and anticipation. The news of the impending departure had woken the soldiers and despite the heavy snow fall they moved with renewed purpose preparing for battle.

The snow continued to fall, getting heavier by the moment. The wind whipped the snow into mini tornados before eventually releasing it so it could settle. A thin crisp white layer soon covered the dirty snow that had weathered the Merthurian's occupation. Through the greyness a lone rider went unnoticed as he directed his Shektar towards the outlying tents.

The giant beast snorted. His hot breath steaming against the chill wind. The rider leaned forward rubbing the neck of the creature attempting to soothe the animal's nerves. The rider whispered in the Shektar's ear. The calming words had the desired effect and the huge animal padded forward between the tents.

There was no purpose to the layout of the great camp. The large tent of Tol-Son-Ray was surrounded by the Red Prime Soldiers, and after that it was a chaotic mixture of auxiliary, cavalry and support troops. Some had grouped together, others had simply pitched their tents where there was space. In the short time that they had been billeted on the ice sheet, natural walkways and thoroughfares had emerged marking the quickest route between the essential services of the canteen and the latrine. So when a makeshift stockade had been required, its location carried the same amount of forethought as the majority of the camp - the next free space. The small prison dome had been situated on the outskirts in amongst some of the cavalry troops.

The lone rider made his way into the periphery of the outpost taking care that his mount did not inadvertently step on any of the domes. As he neared the low entrance to one such tent a soldier appeared drawing his fur coat over his shoulders. He started as he came face to face with the black nose of the Shektar.

"Whoa!" exclaimed the soldier. The Shektar curled its lip and a low growl rumbled in its throat. Once more the rider reached forward to settle the creature.

"I'm sorry" said the rider. "He's always a little bit jumpy around strangers."

The startled guard relaxed a little as he looked up into the face of the Red Prime rider.

"That's fine. No need to apologise. I should have been looking where I was going. I have so much to do before we leave in the morning." The soldier stood to one side allowing the mounted rider past.

"Perhaps you can help me?" asked the rider. "I am looking for the prisoners that were brought in from the citadel. My captain needs to ask them a few questions. I know it was around here somewhere , but in this storm everything looks the same."

"I know what you mean. If it wasn't for the smell I would have a job to the find the washroom" laughed the soldier. "I think it is over to the North. There are quite a few cavalry posted near it, I think. Look, I must get going otherwise I'll never have the supplies ready in time. May the luck of the gods be with you tomorrow brother."

"And with you my friend" smiled the Red Prime rider.

*

Mido opened his eyes. His skull pounded. It felt like a demon was trapped in his mind, beating the walls of his brain in a bid for freedom. He reached to the back of his head and felt the hard mat of hair that had congealed over the wound.

"Mido! You're alive!"

Still blurry from his forced slumber he felt his brother embrace him.

"It's OK Mort. I am fine. Just got the headache of the ages, that's all."

"I thought you were dead" stated Mort.

"Well I'm surprised you didn't steal my jerkin" smiled Mido.

"I was tempted. It's painfully cold" replied his brother.

"What happened to Bron? Have you seen her?"

"Not since we first got here. That murderer Petr took her."

"How long have I been out?" asked Mido.

"One moon at most I think. It's hard to tell from within here, everything is so dark."

The small hide covering the entrance suddenly flipped inwards and light briefly burst into the interior.

"Keep it shut you two, else you'll find yourselves on the menu" came the gruff voice from the guard outside. Mido reached out and felt for his brother. He pulled him close and whispered into his ear.

"We've got to find a way out of here, and get Bron."

"Already on it. The walls are only made of hide, outside of that is heaped snow and ice. I have already made a start." In the dim shadows Mido could see his brother holding up a small sliver of bone. He watched as he crawled to the back of the prison dome and felt for the torn hide. He lifted the flap and continued to slowly and quietly scrape at the ice behind. They both froze as they heard noises from outside. Laughter. They relaxed and continued with their escape.

The two guards at the prison entrance were old friends. They had both been annoyed when they had been detailed guard duty. But now with the forthcoming march, it was the easiest job going.

"I can't believe I complained about this posting" joked Volmir.

"Me neither. The rest of our squad are on food supply duty. I don't fancy sitting around a hole in the ice all day, and then having to gut all those fish."

Both men laughed together. They didn't notice the lone Shektar rider approach them, until he was a breath away.

"What can we do for you?" asked Volmir still smiling.

"I have been sent to get the prisoners. Captain Petr's orders"

"Sure. What does the old war hound want with them?" asked Volmir.

"Who knows?" said the rider "I expect he wants to have some fun with the woman before we set off tomorrow."

"Woman?" queried Volmir. "The captain already has the woman?" His curiosity rising he turned from opening the prison entrance and walked alongside the mounted rider grabbing hold of the creature's reigns. The Shektar snorted and swung his head away from the guard.

"Careful" said the rider. "He bites."

"Just exactly who are you" asked the guard

drawing his sword. The rider turned in his saddle and lent over towards the guard. He ignored the sword tip pointed towards his throat.

"I am the last person you'll ever see" said the rider quietly. As he did, the massive creature swung his head knocking the guard sprawling across the ice. In an instant the Shektar reared upwards and then pounded its two front paws down onto the chest of the flailing soldier. The weight of the creature crushed his ribcage rupturing his heart and lungs. As the rider swung back to face the other guard he saw him drop to his knees a splinter of bone sticking out from his neck. The two brothers stood innocently behind him.

"Var?" asked the brothers in unison.

"Who else?" smiled the rider.

"I thought I recognised your voice. I told you it was him." Mort punched his brother playfully in the shoulder.

"Where's Bron?" asked Var.

"She's not here. Petr took her with him when we arrived" explained Mort.

"Get on" ordered Var. The two brothers clambered up onto the back of the animal as it grunted its disapproval of the extra weight. Var was about to venture back into the camp when he realised his escapade hadn't gone unnoticed. Guards were running from the nearby tents shouting and waking their comrades to the danger.

He kicked his heels into the flanks of the Shektar and urged him forward.

"Come on Hotay, time to show me how fast you can go boy"

The massive beast needed no further encouragement and vaulted out across the ice. In moments the creature and its passengers were lost in the blizzard.

*

The Virtue of Water hurried across to the large group huddled around the gaping hole in the ice. Magta and Dumonii alike all stared expectantly into the dark water. Tol-Aka made his way to the edge of the manmade opening and joined the communal trance. A dark object shimmered just beneath the surface. Light bounced and distorted as the object came closer. Eventually in a shower of water Lothair broke through, gasping for air. The assembled giants hauled the Titan from the freezing water wrapping him in blankets. His skin was blue and he was shaking uncontrollably.

"That was cutting it close. I told you your body would start to break down when exposed to those temperatures" berated Hanelore. Lothair looked up at his father with a defeated expression.

"Well? Did you find them?" asked Hanelore.

"Yes" shivered Lothair. "It is secured. But there is only one." He removed the blanket and fumbled with the knot holding a sturdy rope around his waist. He held one of the ends up to Hanelore.

"Here you go. If you can just pull it up, we'll start searching for the next one." Lothair smiled at his father. Hanelore ignored the jibe and turned to talk with Tol-Aka.

"This is good news" said the Virtue. "We'll need to lift it vertically spreading the weight out across the ice. If we try pulling it up the rope could sever on the ice or worse the ice will give way."

"What did you have in mind?" asked the giant.

"Two 'A' frames and a pulley system should do it. I only hope that when we get it to the surface the ice will hold until we can drag it to the safety of the ruins" replied Tol-Aka.

"Let's find out" said Hanelore already busy organising people and equipment.

Since their exodus from the South and their coalition with the Dumonii, Hanelore had somehow emerged as the overall person in charge. With so many rulers, his oblivious attitude to their accompanying egos was what was called for. A simple direct mind focussed on the plan. A plan that had surprisingly been suggested by the Emperor.

As the convoy had approached the island of Imercia they

had anchored some considerable distance away, unsure of where the Merthurian army would appear next. After scouting the area the huge force was spotted camped to the East of the island. They had convened a council of alliance. After hearing the Emperor's proposition they had wasted no time. Var, The Emperor and his elite Dominators had left for the city of Asturia. They were due back in two moons. In that time the remaining force had to make its way to the ancient ruins of Labna. It was here that they now scoured the shattered city in search of the hallowed stones. None knew if the plan would work, but it was all that they had. If it failed then the alliance would make its last stand at Labna. With one day rapidly fading and only 4 of the 5 stones discovered, that now looked like more of a certainty.

Ruins of the once great civilisations were dotted all around the globe. Some had been lost forever but those that had been constructed in the high mountain ranges had survived. Until recent history the few that remained had spent their existence beneath the ocean waves. The speed at which the sea levels rose had preserved much of the architecture. The resultant seasons submerged had eroded the finer detail with the corals and creatures making a permanent home on the man-made structures. As the sea levels now dropped once again, the encrusted buildings were released from their silent tomb and thrust into the noisy icy world above.

Part of the ancient city of Labna still remained under the

pack ice, but two considerable areas stood clear of the surrounding snowscape. The buildings had been built on prominent peaks and the city had occupied these and the expanse in-between.

In its forgotten history this had once been a Dumonii city. On their arrival Tol-Aka had quickly identified key locations on the peaks explaining the typical layout of a city. His knowledge and that of his Principles had located the building they were after in the first afternoon. Two of the stones had been standing in the same place that they were erected millennia ago. The structure in which they stood had collapsed down the steep hillside and they found a third stone buried under rubble on this slope. Lothair had just discovered the fourth lying in the ocean at the base of the slope. Of the fifth stone there was no sign.

It was first light before they were ready to lift the fourth stone. They had worked into the night to construct the huge wooden frames that they needed. They had cannibalised the main masts of the ice yachts for the contraption. As the first rays of the great star broke the horizon, Tol-Aka signalled to the long line of giants to pick up the rope.

"The pulley is attached" shouted the Virtue. "We just need brute force now"

"We have plenty of that" said Hanelore.

The Magta picked up the rope and dug their heels into the ice, chipping away to make footholds along its length. The giants grunted as they felt the weight of the stone for the first time. Slowly but steadily they moved back across the ice. The ocean was relatively shallow this close into the ruins and it wasn't long before the old stone emerged. It cracked through the thin ice sheet that had re-formed over the opening. As it cleared the water, the surrounding Dumonii fed wooden poles beneath it whilst another group now pulled it to one side.

Hanelore signalled to the Magta to slacken the rope. The mighty stone was slowly lowered onto its makeshift sled. The wooden poles and the ice creaked and groaned under the colossal weight, but it held firm. The assembled workers wasted no time in dragging the stone to the edge of the ice.

A cheer went up. Any small victory was welcomed.

"What now?" asked Tol-Aka.

Hanelore looked reluctantly across at the hole as the broken slabs of ice knocked against each other.

"It makes sense that the last stone is under there somewhere" he said.

"It's not there" interjected Lothair.

"I know you don't want to go back again my son, but without Var one of us must go. The Dumonii would die within moments, it has to be one of us" explained Hanelore.

"I'll go" came a voice from behind.

"You should be resting brother" said the Titan.

"Pah!" spat Gero. "Plenty of time for that later. If we don't find that stone then Var might as well lead his people into that hole. Besides, I need to get away from this nursemaid." Gero indicated to the small Medicator that stood by his side. "I'm sure that's one place he won't follow me."

Lothair placed his hand on his brother's shoulder.

"It's good to see you brother. I'm sorry..."

"It's just history" interrupted Gero. "Which we'll all be if we don't stop talking."

Lothair laughed.

"Perhaps you can check the building at the top of the hill. You may see something we have missed. You seem to have a knack for finding that which has been lost." Lothair placed his forehead against his brother's. This time Gero did not pull away.

Gero scrambled up the rock strewn hillside slipping on the snow in his eagerness to get to the top. The Medicator desperately tried to keep pace. The giant soon left him behind. After some considerable effort the Dumonii healer reached the summit. Gero was slumped against the base of pillar breathing heavily.

"You're not ready for physical exertion yet" puffed the Medicator. "Here let me look at the wound. You need your tablets."

Despite Gero's incredible strength and resilience, the blow he suffered from his brother's wayward hammer blow would have killed him if not for the skill and knowledge of the Dumonii. The strike had crushed his ribcage and his ribs had punctured his lungs. Even with their knowledge of herbs and drugs the injury was beyond the knowledge of the Magta. The Emperor had suggested that one of his Medicators could operate and try to fix the wound. After much protest from Hanelore and Lothair they had agreed to the otherworldly surgery.

They had watched as the Medicator had cut into the giant's abdomen. He had removed some of the broken ribs and wired others back together. He had made repairs to Gero's lungs before eventually closing the incision. The gathered Magta were amazed by the process, sceptical of its success, but amazed nonetheless. Since the operation the Medicator had remained at Gero's side administering a foul smelling poultice to the wound and ensuring that the unco-operative giant took his prescribed drink and medication.

Much to Gero's astonishment the injury had healed well. Scar tissue now tore a red line across his stomach, but it was clean and clear of infection. Black stitches still criss-crossed the wound and it felt tight each time he breathed. The procedure had saved his life, of that he had no doubt.

The Medicator pulled a roll bag from within his coat and laid it out on the floor. He thumbed the various bottles and then pulled one from its securing loop. Popping two of the pills into his palm, he handed them to the giant. Gero took the tablets and swallowed them.

"How long before these start working" asked Gero.

"As I have said, the road to recovery is not simple. The wound on your stomach may have healed well, but your lungs will take longer. They need time to repair themselves."

"I just felt a bit breathless after climbing that hill" complained Gero. "I need a bit of exercise to get air back into my lungs. I am feeling better already." Gero stood.

"You must rest, please just stay a while longer" pleaded the Medicator.

"Nonsense" grumbled Gero. "Here look at this."

Gero bent down and circled his arms around a broken piece of column. Leaning back he lifted the massive piece of stone off the floor. He readjusted his grip before thrusting the masonry up into the air. Pain flared in his side and the giant dropped the stone backwards. As it crashed to the floor it shattered the flagstone. Snow and rubble poured into the void below. Ignoring the pain Gero brushed away the ice and debris and stared down into the large chamber.

"Give me your coat" demanded Gero.

The Medicator obliged and handed the eager giant his outer fur. He watched in disbelief as Gero struck his flint into the garment. After several attempts smoke wisped up, and after three shallow breaths, fire engulfed the coat. Gero dropped the flaming material into the pit. It hit the floor in a puff of embers and the flickering flame slowly illuminated the hidden crypt. At one end of the room was a massive altar. It consisted of one huge stone with a deep spiral cut into its surface. Gero turned to the Medicator and smiled.

"Looks like we've found number five."

*

The Emperor was waiting at the postern gate as Var led his Shektar carrying the two brothers up the steep incline.

"Partial success?" asked the Emperor.

"Yes" replied Var. "My brothers are fine; bruised and cold, but fine. There was no sign of Bron. Petr is keeping her close to him, so I didn't get a chance to look further."

"Will you go back again this night?"

"I wish I could but we are out of time. They are mobilising as we speak. They march in the morning. I cannot jeopardise all our lives for the sake of one person, no matter how much my heart aches."

The Emperor could see the overwhelming sadness in Var's eyes.

"He will not kill her, she has worth. There will be another chance."

Var needed to change the subject.

"How is the evacuation going?"

"Those who were able and those who wanted to leave are already out on the ice. They should make it to the ruins by first light if they travel through the night." The Emperor paused. Var could see he was struggling with something.

"What is it?" asked Var.

"Your mother is one of those who refuses to leave" answered the Emperor. "The death of your father has crushed her will. I think you may need to speak with her. I will take your brothers with me, we leave now. I will see you at Labna my friend."

Var looked up at the Emperor. That was the first time he had used that term. Var clenched him by the wrist.

"I'll see you at first light."

*

Var climbed the spiral staircase in the keep and made his way to his parents' room. He tapped lightly on the door. There was no reply. He turned the door hoop and slowly made his way inside. His mother sat in the window looking out over the harbours. He made his way to her. He moved a cushion and joined his mother in quiet reflection. The city was deserted. He could just make out the firebrands of the departing population as they disappeared into the gloom. It seemed like only yesterday that the oceans had flowed into the harbour and he and Gero had escaped the politics of rule, whiling away the hours fishing and dreaming. The burden of leadership seemed to increase in weight with the rise of every moon.

"I'm not leaving Var. I know that's why you are here" said his mother.

"I know" said Var solemnly.

"I wish I could stay with you. I wish I could forget about everything, all of my responsibility. Just leave it all behind. I'm so tired mother. There are hundreds of people out there relying on me. I have given them hope that there is an end to all this. I'm not even sure myself any more. I worry I have given them false hope. What if there is no gate? And what if the gods do not exist?"

His mother moved beside him and held his hands in hers.

"It is the sign of a great man, that at his lowest point he can still muster the courage to continue. To stand tall and look fate in the eye, and not yield. That alone is an inspiration to us all."

"I don't know if I am that man" answered Var.

"Yes you do my dear. You have always known it." said Muadin.

A single tear rolled down Var's face. He wiped it clear. As he did he felt the cloud of depression hanging over his shoulders wither away and die. He became aware of his heart beating within his chest and the flicker of the fire that motivated him rekindle. Hope had returned. He stood and turned to leave. His mother held onto his hand.

"When you find him" she said simply.

"I promise" he replied.

*

"Any sign of him yet?" asked Gero.

"No not yet" replied the Emperor.

The last of the ocean tribes had filtered into the makeshift bastion during the night. Those that could fight were now stationed in the rock strewn hills on Labna. The defenders had moved enormous amounts of masonry and piled it high in the valley between the two outcrops. They had positioned it in such a way that the advancing army would be funnelled into a small opening. They hoped that the Merthurian advantage in numbers would be reduced at this choke point. Archers and ocean tribes with harpoons manned the newly created walls. The Dumonii Reavers and Missionrai waited behind the barricade whilst the shield wall of the Magta Destructors stood firm at the centre. The Emperor and his Dominators had taken up position at the front of one of the hills. They had secluded themselves underneath a large sheet covered with snow. They would wait for the enemy to pass before ploughing into their flanks.

As defensible positions went it was as good as any. The thin ice to the North and South would prevent any major force from attacking the rear. They would have no choice but to run into the gaping mouth of the alliance.

At the centre of the Magta lines stood Lothair and Gero. Gero flinched as he rotated his shoulder trying to loosen his arm. Lothair cast him a look of concern.

"Don't even think about talking me out of it" blurted Gero.

"There's no-one I would rather have standing at my side" smiled Lothair.

"Well that's good" grumbled Gero. "But just make sure you keep that cursed hammer pointed away from me this time."

Both giants looked up as they caught a glimpse of something in the distance. As the distortion of distance and the ice diminished they could make out the bounding white creature hurtling towards them. As the rider came closer, the ice beneath their feet started to shake.

"One rider can't be causing that?" said Gero.

"I don't think that's just one rider brother" replied Lothair.

All across the horizon the snow swirled and the grey light of morning seemed to twist, moving, continually moving, getting faster and faster as the Merthurian horde broke into view. Hundreds upon hundreds of mounted riders followed by a sea of fur clad soldiers. Out at the front they could see Var. Standing up in his stirrups, moving his weight in time with his Shektar he rode as if the wind itself carried him.

Within moments Var was pulling on the reigns of Hotay. The giant animal dug its claws into the ice trying to halt its slide towards the Magta. Stopping just short the Shektar sent a wave of ice fragments clattering against the shield wall. Var leapt from the saddle and was about to make his way to his friends when Hotay nudged him with his head.

"Yes of course! How could I forget?" said Var. He stroked the long nose and scratched the huge beast behind its ear. Hotay growled with pleasure and then shook his head vigorously side to side covering Var in saliva. He wiped his face and ran to the front lines.

"Nothing like leaving it to the last minute" complained Gero.

"Good to see you too" replied Var. "I thought it best that I get their attention, just in case they changed their minds." He had to shout now as the rumble of the army coming towards them drowned him out. "Is everything ready?"

"We'll know soon enough" replied Lothair.

"What did Tol-Aka say about the distance?" asked Var.

"Apparently distance makes little difference. The closer they are the more focussed the result but spaced out they should still work the same. It may have unfortunate consequences at the other side" said Gero. "Hopefully" he added.

The huge force of the Merthurian raced headlong towards the defenders. Unperturbed by the defensive situation they were confident in their supremacy. That was until the out flanking riders suddenly crashed through the ice. The giant beasts flailed and howled as they plummeted into the icy water.

The alliance had worked tirelessly through the night hacking away at the ice. Removing huge chunks at a time they created two channels out through the ice. They had refrozen in the early morning but not enough to hold the weight of a Shektar. They had left an ice bridge in the centre further restricting the army into a strangle point.

The giant furred animals thrashed at the edge of the channel trying to pull themselves from the freezing grip of the ocean. Most riders had been thrown as the ice broke. Some were lucky enough to be thrown clear across to the other side but most now batted the water helplessly as the cold shock embraced them. Those that didn't succumb immediately were torn to shreds by their own animals desperate to escape.

Tol-Aka watched the carnage unfold from his vantage point on top of the hill. As the charge faltered at the hidden chasm he signalled across the valley. The five massive stones they had urgently retrieved had been spaced out in the valley. There were two on either side of the walls that made up the funnel and the last stood in front of the giants at the centre.

On seeing the Virtue's signal the Dumonii assigned to each stone started their chants. Their tonal chords slowly awoke the Lexan stone. Each stone started to vibrate and its core began to glow. As the incantation pitch increased so did the intensity of the stones. They hummed as if alive.

Var and the Magta watched as the brightness grew from the five stones.

"This is going to be close" proffered Var.

The red stripes of the front riders could now be clearly seen thundering towards their position. Var mounted Hotay once more. He drew one of his cleavers and wrapped the reigns tightly around his other hand. He looked back at Gero.

"Lead my people to the gates my friend. I will join you as soon as I can" shouted Var.

Gero looked briefly confused before he realised what Var was proposing to do.

"No!" hollered the giant.

Before he had a chance to stop him Var spurred Hotay forward. Gero unhitched his butterfly axe and made to follow. Lothair placed a firm hand on his shoulder.

"This is one fight you can't help with" said his brother.

"The depths I can't!" cursed Gero shaking his brother's hand free.

"Trust me brother this is not your fight" pleaded Lothair. Gero span and squared up to the Titan.

"Listen brother. He is my friend. If he has chosen to risk everything, then I have no problem risking all that I have as well. Death comes for us all brother. At least this way I will meet it on my terms."

The giant sprinted after Var, towards the oncoming army.

From his camouflaged position the Emperor could see ranks of mounted riders pass him. He looked back into the funnel. He saw Var racing to meet the army head on. He saw Gero following some way behind.

"What are they doing?" gasped Bela-Sem.

The Emperor scanned the Merthurian riders. In the centre he could see Var's reason. The Red Prime Captain had

Bronsur strapped across the neck of his mount. She was bound and gagged and was being buffeted by the animal's movement.

Var was hunched over Hotay's head, using his legs to take all of the movement of the Shektar. With his right hand he slashed at the approaching rider's lance, splitting the shaft in two. The strike threw the soldier off balance and as he lilted to one side Var's sword cleaved his head from his shoulders. Var looked ahead. He locked eyes with his nemesis. He gritted his teeth but before he could unleash his next strike his vision blurred and the world as he knew it ended.

At that point the plan unfolded. The stones reached fever pitch and a portal burst into existence. Light exploded from the centre of the Merthurian ranks and the air twisted and buckled under the pressure of the gateway. In one instant thousands of bewildered soldiers vanished. Those outside the portal had no idea what they were seeing and continued their charge into the abyss.

The Emperor turned to his Dominators.

"Follow the instructions of Tol-Aka. I have something I must do" said Lord Vas.

"My Lord?" questioned Bela-Sem.

Before he could ask another question the Emperor ran from their hiding place and sprinted towards the bucking gateway. The Dominators looked at each other and in silent agreement all started to follow after their Emperor. Before they could make it onto the sea ice the portal crackled and popped, the energy it contained collapsed on itself and as quickly as it had opened the gate closed.

The expanse of nothing that now remained where the army had been was too hard for some to comprehend. The rear guard of the Merthurian army faltered as they stumbled into the open space. They stood staring all around looking for any sign of their mighty army. All they saw and heard was the oncoming charge of the Magta.

Chapter 3 - Stranded

Hotay came to an abrupt stop sending Var headlong into the sea of Merthurian warriors. He landed heavily managing to absorb the impact by rolling on his shoulder. He found himself surrounded by Shektar. Some rearing into the air, others twisting and turning, all of them as confused as their riders by the sudden change of situation and environment.

Above the chaotic milling of soldiers and beasts one voice thundered out. Toll-Son-Ray barked orders at all those around him, trying to establish a foothold of sanity. Var remained crouched. The soldiers had ignored him until now, but it wouldn't take long before order and memory were restored.

Var darted through the legs of one huge beast. He emerged and sprinted towards his goal. The giant animals buffeted him from side to side as their riders fought to calm their steeds. In the jolt from the icy reality of Gebshu many of the riders had been unseated. Many had lost the grip on their reigns and followed a similar path to Var plummeting into the mass of the Merthurian force. Some were not so lucky and had splintered bones as they landed. Others were now being trampled by clawed paws.

Var threw a supply sack to one side as he searched through the debris. His heart pounded in his chest as he saw the blood soaked hair of the crumpled person in front of him. He knelt down and gently rolled the body over. Bronsur's eyes flicked open.

"I'm sorry" she whispered.

A single tear trickled down Var's cheek.

"Without you there is no destiny worth fighting for" he replied. He placed his arms under hers and helped her up. Bronsur's legs buckled as she tried to stand. Var sheathed his swords and then lifted Bronsur over his shoulder. He turned looking for a route out of the throng. As his mind rapidly evaluated the choices he noticed a Shektar purposefully manoeuvre to block his path. Var looked up into the red striped face of Petr.

"I wondered what happened to my passenger" said the rider. "If you'd just like to hand her over." The captain slowly lowered his polearm, levelling it at Var's chest.

"I feel I must compliment you on your plan. I have no idea where we have ended up, but judging by this unknown city I am assuming we are a long way from home. Tell me Var. It is Var isn't it? Asked Petr. Var remained silent.

"Was this also part of your plan - ride in alone and rescue your loved one?" Petr laughed. "I admire your bravery, but there is a fine line between bravery and stupidity." Before the Red Prime captain could continue his gloating he was thumped back off his mount as a huge butterfly axe slammed into his chest.

"There is also a fine line between confidence and arrogance" grumbled Gero as he appeared behind Var. Var smiled.

"I didn't mean for you to be here Gero. This was something I just had to do" explained Var.

"It's not just me" answered Gero. "Looks like you have made another friend." Gero indicated over his shoulder towards Lord Vas who was making his way towards them.

"This way" said the Emperor.

The group quickly made their way through the continually moving mass of soldiers and out across into the city suburbs. With the attention of the Red Prime captain removed they passed unhindered away from the Merthurian army. The Emperor led them through a double doorway and into a dark storage room where they paused for breath. Var lowered Bronsur softly onto the floor. He moved some grain sacks so that she sat upright. He cupped her bloody face in his hands.

"I won't be a moment. There is one other person we have forgotten."

Var walked back to the open doorway. He put two fingers in his mouth and then whistled. He repeated the action scanning the streets ahead. He was about to try for a third time when he noticed the white animal bounding towards him. He waited by the door as the massive Shektar approached. Hotay snorted on his arrival. Var reached up grabbing the reigns. He smoothed the animal as he led it inside.

"Well done boy" Var soothed. Hotay muscled his way past Gero and after circling for a couple of times finally settled down in the corner of the room.

"Well at least someone is making themselves at home" complained Gero. "And talking of home, does anyone know where we are?"

"We are in Sagen-Ita" answered the Emperor.

"And that is where exactly?" asked the giant.

"This is.... This was my home. Sagen-Ita is the sacred capital of Son-Gebshu. I made my last stand here in the war of the Virtues, before I was forced to your world."

"Well it looks like the Virtues are going to have their hands full for a while" suggested Var nodding towards the Merthurian who were now assembling into more ordered ranks.

"If you left here and made it to Gebshu, then surely we can do the same?" said Gero.

"I had all of the known gates destroyed. The main gate inside the temple which we used to travel to Gebshu was rigged to implode as soon as it closed" replied the

Emperor.

"A brilliant plan!" said Gero. Vas turned on the giant, in one smooth move drawing his knife and holding it up to Gero's throat.

"Know this Magta, I would have gladly died defending my people here. I still carry that scar of defeat, do not think to make light of it."

Gero lifted his arm slowly placing a single finger on top of the Emperor's blade. He pushed it slowly downwards.

"You are swift to anger Dumon" replied Gero. "We now find ourselves stranded on this moon. Those friends and family who now make their way to the Pillars of Itna, will do so in vain if we cannot return Var. He holds the hope for all our lives including that of your people. It is time to put senseless pride to one side."

"Pride!" growled the Emperor. "It is not self-admiration that drives me you fool. It is duty. Just as Var must fulfil his birthright, I have a duty to my people. For revolutions my forebears had squandered our resources and our knowledge. I wanted a future for my people, just as you do for your own kind, and I would have sacrificed everything to achieve it."

"We all want the same thing" said Var. "But we can do without fighting each other to get it. Bron is hurt, we need to get her some help. The Mer and the Virtues will be occupied with each other for the time being. We should use this time and try to find a way home. Whatever happens between them, neither is going to welcome us with open arms."

Gero glared at the Emperor before turning his back and making his way to the door.

"Vas, we don't have much time, where can we get help for Bron?" asked Var.

The Emperor walked towards Bronsur and knelt beside her.

"She is too weak to move" said the Emperor. "Look after her here as best you can. I will go and fetch help. It is better if I go alone." The Emperor rose and walked to join Gero in the doorway. "I do not know if there are other gates, or if the knowledge still exists to forge a new gateway. There is however someone who might. When I return we will make our way to find him, if he still lives."

The Emperor drew his two war hammers and ran out into the city streets.

"I don't trust him" muttered Gero.

*

Principle Tar-Ota paused at the ornate doors set into the massive bulwark of Tower Wall. He had run from the lower city and the lack of exercise was taking its toll. The two gate guards watched on in amusement as the Principle struggled to voice his orders.

"Shut the gate" he stammered.

Tar-Ota took a deep breath and then continued his journey towards the Royal Palace. The imposing keep tower rose up above its protective walls like a great stone god. Tattered flags and pennants hung along its facade like some gaudy necklace. The opulence of the outer and inner wards had fallen rapidly into decay, and the once magnificent palace could now sit mournfully alongside the buildings in the city slums.

The exhausted Principle clung to the balustrade as he reached the top of the final staircase. He wiped the sweat from his brow and attempted to straighten his gowns. The luxurious purple fabric that had once strained to contain his ample stomach now hung loosely on his thin frame. His composure regained, he walked towards the Royal Chamber and the guards obliged by opening the aureate doors. As they opened, the cool perfumed air inside the chamber washed over the drained Principle revitalising his senses. He walked quietly into the room towards the two men sat opposite each other. They were lost in concentration, all attention focused on the fastidiously carved playing pieces set out in front of them. The larger man moved his hand and left it tentatively hovering over a green jewelled piece. He looked up at his opponent. A mean smile appeared across his face. The rotund man quickly withdrew his hand. His concentration momentarily broken he looked at Tar-Ota with accusing eyes.

"I thought I said absolutely no interruptions. It

looks like you have cost me this game." blurted the Virtue of Earth.

"Don't be ridiculous Frey. I had this game wrapped up shortly after we started this morning. Don't blame poor Tar-Ota" said Alu-Aka.

"I'm sorry my Lords" started Tar-Ota. "I would not have bothered you if it were not of the utmost importance."

"What can be that urgent? If the citizens are complaining about the rationing again then just hang a few of them from the Pinnacle Wall. That will stop their bleating" said Frey-Aka.

The Virtue of Air recognised the look of anguish on the face of the Principle.

"What is it? asked Alu-Aka.

"It is probably best that I show you" replied Tar-Ota. "If you would kindly accompany me to the Ascension Gate, you will be able to see from there."

The Virtue of Air stood up quickly, knocking the playing board and scattering the priceless counters across the marble floor.

"Tell me what is going on" demanded Alu-Aka grabbing hold of the surprised Principle.

"An army has appeared in the lower city..."

"An army! What are you talking about? How can an army get into the city?" asked Frey-Aka.

"Let him finish" shouted Alu-Aka releasing his grip. The overwhelmed Principle looked at the expectant faces of the two Virtues.

"An army has appeared in the lower city. I do not know how. It looked like gate warp when they arrived, but I cannot be sure. They are like nothing I have ever seen before. They are riding huge white furred animals, and there are hundreds of them, maybe thousands. It is hard to tell. They have gathered in the open space of the city arena" explained Tar-Ota.

"Is he with them?" asked Frey-Aka.

"I do not believe he is. Their leader has already made himself known and he is definitely not the Emperor, I mean the Nameless."

"Have they made any demands?" asked Alu-Aka.

The Principle paused. He took a deep breath.

"They asked to speak with someone in authority. Gem-Ota was at the Hall of Learning so he went out to meet them. They conversed for some time but without provocation their leader thrust his spear right through the neck of Gem-Ota. The population panicked. Those who could have made it behind the Last Bastion. I ordered all gates to be lowered from there to the Tower Wall."

"Gem-Ota was never the best orator. It looks like your silver tongue is required" said Frey-Aka.

"We will see my friend. Ensure every Reaver and Missionrai that can hold a weapon is called to arms. Post them evenly from the Ascension Gate to our position here at the Palace. Whoever they are, we will break their bones as they flounder and die upon our great defences."

"What about the Last Bastion and the Pinnacle Wall? Are we not going to defend them?" asked Tar-Ota in confusion.

"We are. But I do not want to waste what troops we have unnecessarily. Have the Missionrai supply arms and basic armour to the populace. They can earn their food for once. They will defend the lower city. Make it known that by royal decree no-one without a name may pass beyond the Ascension gate. They must stand and fight."

"They will stand and die" pleaded Tar-Ota.

"They will. And with them our food shortage problem. If they can take some of the aggressors with them, then all the better. Fetch me my armour" demanded Alu-Aka.

The royal city of Sagen-Ita, although a shadow of its former glory was the most formidable fortress ever constructed by the Dumonii. It was built on the Island of Hope which lay a short distance from the shore in the Sea of Serenity. It had been the ancestral home of the Emperor since the very first migration.

The island had precipitous rocky cliffs protecting it on all sides. Three harbours provided the only access to the main city and this was only along steep narrow steps all sheltered by towers and defensive walls. The Dumonii had engineered a series of great walls that led up the temple mount. The first of these was called 'The Last Bastion'. Behind this the 'Pinnacle Wall' protected the impressive Hall of Justice and the gateway to the Bridge of Lies. Gargantuan amounts of stone had been removed from the island to form a manmade canyon separating the lower city from the upper temple court. At one end of this bridge stood the Ascension Gate. These twin towers dwarfed the lower gateway and despite their lower situation on the hillside they countered the height of the Royal Palace way above.

Crossing the upper city was the 'Tower Wall'. Five massive defensive pillars blocking the route into the Outer Ward. Inside this stood the Royal Palace and the Inner Ward, both menacing citadels in their own right. Finally inside the Inner Ward stood the oldest of all the Dumonii temples, Ro-Mor.

A defending force with enough numbers could easily hold each wall indefinitely. The Last Bastion had been breached only twice in its ancient history. Once only due to a treacherous Principle and the second time during the recent War of the Virtues. The defending army of Emperor

Vas was so depleted in numbers it was unable to adequately man the walls, and after a desperate resistance the Tower Wall fell to the invading armies of the Virtue of Earth, Air and Fire.

Although this was an immeasurable victory for the Virtues the ramifications of the civil war were far reaching. The resources needed to feed, clothe and arm the masses were robbed from conquered towns and villages. Those places not destroyed in the fighting were left derelict as the denizens moved in search of food. The majority of the great cities and temples of Son-Gebshu now lay deserted as people had abandoned their homes and made their way to Sagen-Ita. The population of the capital now swelled to four times its pre-civil war number. Overcrowded and overpromised the salvation that those who followed the Virtues had hoped for, never materialised.

The vast food ziggurats that the last Emperor had sought to re-introduce had been hastily repaired and cleansed but the harvests continued to fail. Temperatures dropped, and the light from Shu even at the height of summer was not enough to ripen the crops.

What food there was had to be rationed. Hundreds now lay dying through starvation and disease. Dissent had crept into the population and even into the ranks of the Reavers and Missionrai. The price of victory had been too high.

*

Vas kept to the dark corners of the city as he made his way towards the prison complex. In the upheaval the arrival of the Merthurian army had caused, the streets were deserted, but Vas couldn't take any chances in being recognised. At least not now.

The Last Bastion gate was closed but as most residents of the city knew the huge defensive walls that surrounded the entire city were all linked. Not enough for an invading army to take advantage of but enough for one man to slip through unnoticed.

The main prison and holding cells were situated at the top of the East Harbour steps. They had been built by tunnelling deep into the bedrock of the island. A single entry point led down to a guard room and a Medicator station. Attaching a medical facility to a penal facility was common practice for the Dumonii. The concept was not to protect the wellbeing of prisoners, exactly the opposite was true. The Medicators ensured the torture victims survived for the longest possible time. Their surgeries and countermeasures only served to prolong the pain.

Vas listened. He could hear two separate voices coming from the guard room below. With his back to the wall he slid down the stairs. The two guards were standing in the centre of the room arguing. Behind them was what looked like a Medicator. He was slumped in a chair, fast asleep. The two men ceased their quarrel as the figure of the

Emperor loomed into the room.

"You.." The recognition of the nearest guard ended abruptly as the Emperor's war hammer split his skull asunder. The second guard fell backwards his hand still firmly clasped around his sword hilt. Blood seeped from a square hole ruptured in his temple. The commotion had not woken the Medicator. Vas thrust a kick downwards splintering the chair legs and sending the man skittering across the floor. Before the small balding man had a chance to rub the sleep from his eyes the Emperor had hoisted him from the floor. His feet now dangled freely as Vas brought him to his own eye level.

"Praise the Gods!" yelled the Medicator. "I knew you would return to save us all."

"What is your name?" asked the Emperor.

"My name is Ben-l. I did not want to oppose you honest. I just did what I was ordered to do. They would have killed me. I am so glad to see you. I will happily serve your army against those traitorous Virtues. I have some skills as a Medicator" babbled Ben-l.

"You have finished?" said the Emperor.

"Well if you want references..." continued Ben-l.

"No" said the Emperor firmly. "You have finished. Retrieve your medical kit. I have need of your ability. Oh, and from now on you will not speak. Is that clear?"

The Medicator nodded rapidly. Vas lowered him to the floor and watched him nervously collect his medical belongings. As the Emperor looked on he heard a weak cough coming from the long passage towards the cells.

"Is anyone being held here?" asked the Emperor. Again the Medicator nodded furiously. "Come with me."

The damp dark corridor led out into a circular chamber. The room was surrounded by small barred holding cells. A further walkway led down to a similar chamber. The layout repeated itself way down into the bowels of the island.

In one of the cells was a prone semi-naked body. Vas moved to the cage and shook the metal door. The noise caused the captive to lift his head. His right eye was closed over due to bruising, his lips were freshly cut and the rest of his face showed the scars and burn marks of his time in detention. His body mirrored his broken visage. Rough scars, some healed some still with crude stitching, all covered in dried blood mixed with the grime and dirt of the cell floor criss-crossed his tortured flesh. He had tattoos covering his upper body, but there were blank patches which had been replaced by angry raised scar tissue. Vas recognised the design. This man was a Dominator. The emblems of the Emperor that were incorporated into his tattoo had been cut from his skin.

Vas stepped back and with a vicious swing the lock bounced onto the floor. Vas knelt by the man and helped him to sit.

"My Lord?" stammered the Dominator. He looked around the room at Ben-I. "What kind of trick is this?"

"This is no trick my friend. Can you walk?" asked Vas.

"I can damn well walk out of here." He allowed the Emperor to assist him as he stood. He suddenly reached forward drawing the Emperor's knife from his belt.

"Get back. You are a lie!" sneered the Dominator through his broken teeth.

"No my friend It is I, Vas. Despite your current demeanour I would recognise you anywhere Gav-Sem. Now give me back my blade, we have work to do. I am assuming you wish to resume your role as a Dominator?"

The shocked expression on Gav-Sem's face faded and for the first time in a revolution a smile appeared.

"Yes my Lord" said Gav-Sem attempting to stand as straight as his injured body would allow. The Emperor strode back into the guard room followed by his two new companions. He turned to the Dominator and placed a hand on his shoulder.

"Take their clothes and arm yourself, I can't have you catching a cold." said the Emperor. He then turned to Ben-I. "Who?" he asked simply. The small Medicator knew exactly what he was asking.

"The Virtue of Air" he replied.

The Emperor nodded.

*

Var held his canteen to Bronsur's lips. She sipped the ice cold water. Var saw tears well in her eyes.

"We're here now. There's no sense dwelling on the past. We all make bad decisions sometimes. I should know, I am the master of poor decision making. Anyway you know how much Gero and I love adventuring."

"I thought he would listen. I thought I could save the bloodshed. Instead we are stranded here and I have brought destruction to another civilisation" explained Bronsur.

"Well I wouldn't worry about these people, they had it coming" smiled Var.

"Not all of them" came a stern voice from the doorway. As the silhouetted figure entered the room the light slowly revealed his horrific features. Var shrunk back from the scarred man.

"Do not concern yourself. I have always been this good looking" said Gav-Sem.

The Emperor then entered dragging a small man with him. He pointed at Bronsur and the Medicator nodded quickly attending to the wounded woman.

"This is Gav-Sem. He is one of my Dominators and can be trusted. As soon as the woman is ready to travel he will show you a way to the Northern Harbour. You may have to persuade someone to lend you a boat, but I am sure that is within your capability. I will meet you at first light tomorrow morning. If I am not there, then Gav-Sem will know what to do."

"What about you? What are you going to do?" asked Var.

"I have something that I left unfinished. May the Gods grant us favour." With that the Emperor disappeared once more.

With introductions made and Ben-I applying what treatment he could to both Bronsur and Gav-Sem, the group made their way out from their hiding place for the first time since their abrupt arrival. The Merthurian army had surprisingly left most of the city intact and were busy re-organising their forces. They seemed in no hurry and had made the green open space of the city arena into a makeshift camp.

Gav-Sem led the strange band of individuals along the Eastern wall until they came to a small ladder. It had been crudely lashed together and leant at a steep angle against the huge wall. The Dominator signalled to climb. One by one they made their way up onto the defensive structure. The ladder creaked and bowed, as it strained under Gero's bulk, but it held to allow him to join the others.

"We shouldn't meet any resistance, perhaps not until we get to Cruel Point. The tower there can be shut off from the lower city. I expect it is locked tight. Unfortunately it is the only way out to the harbour" said the Dominator.

They crossed several lookout towers unimpeded but as predicted the small door into the harbour gatehouse was barred. To their right over the wall was a sheer drop down the rocky cliff and into the sea. To their right would lead them back into the lower city where Red Prime soldiers were busy checking each and every dwelling. The round tower in front was made from smooth stone, and the joins in the masonry were minute. Even if there were handholds the tower soared high above them.

"Any ideas?" asked Var.

"Mind your backs!" shouted Gero from behind. The group spun to see the giant running towards them holding a massive piece of stone above his head. As he reached them he launched it forwards. The huge block smashed the door off its hinges and disappeared into the interior. Gero swept his hands together removing the dust.

"My stone key has yet to fail me" he smiled.

The tower was empty. The lower main doors had been locked and then barricaded with every heavy item that could be found. The defenders had left personal items scattered everywhere in the rush to leave. Var stepped over the mess and ventured out towards the connecting bridge. Cruel Point was a small island separated from the mainland by a thin strip of water. The Dumonii had connected the two pieces of land via an arched stone bridge. At the other side of the bridge was a smaller tower and the steps down to the harbour. The vast majority of boats had already left and could be seen bobbing their way to the mainland. A few were still being loaded.

"We must have a boat. Without it we cannot get to the Emperor" said Gav-Sem.

"And that is a bad thing because.." added Gero.

"Because without the Emperor you are stuck on this moon" growled the Dominator.

"That makes sense" said Gero winking at Var. "Let's get ourselves some transport shall we."

"First we need to cross this!" shouted Var.

As the Dumonii had retreated they had destroyed the centre section of the bridge. A gap the length of two men now opened up to reveal the white caps of the waves below breaking in the thin gorge. Gero joined Var on the edge of the break and both stared down into the water.

"Leap of faith" suggested Var.

"I think so" replied Gero. The giant turned and surveyed the confused group. "You'll do" said Gero sweeping the Medicator off the floor. "It's nothing personal. It is just you are the smallest, except Bron maybe, but then she is injured." Gero smiled at Bronsur.

Var came running back from the tower clutching a coil of rope. He secured it around Ben-l's waist and nodded at the giant.

"Relax. The landing will hurt a lot less" explained Gero. He grabbed the panicking Medicator and gripping the rope at the knot ran towards the gap. As he neared he twisted his upper torso and catapulted the screaming man out across the divide. The flailing Dumonii missile cleared the opening and landed heavily on the other side. Gero looked back and winced at the others. They watched as the meagre Medicator slowly picked himself up and dusted off his clothes. He turned back to the giant.

"What's stopping me untying this and leaving you all there?" shouted Ben-l.

Gero just lifted up the rope and nodded towards it.

"I could have you back over this side as quickly as you left. I can do this as many times as you like" said the giant. "I'll feed you some slack and then loop it around one of the crennellations several times. That should be enough to hold it."

Resigned to his fate the Medicator did as he was asked and was soon joined by Var and then the rest of the group shimmied across. They wasted no more time and hurried down the stone steps and out onto the harbour wall. There were several boats left but all had varying levels of water inside them. The fleeing Dumonii had expedited their escape as they had seen the group approaching. The nearest boat was now a couple lengths from the end of the protective barrier.

Var pointed down into the harbour at the rusting seablade. Water could be seen sloshing around inside the cabin, but it wasn't completely scuttled.

"That thing will never get us there. We'll all drown" pleaded Ben-I.

"It only has to do a short trip" laughed Var as he vaulted onto the crumbling hulk. Gero followed him and his weight dented the metal plates where he landed.

"Wait here!" Var yelled to his companions up above. He dived into the cabin. Var held his hands together in prayer as he primed the starter. The old machine coughed several times as the long unused engine cleared the debris from its exhaust. The seablade finally started and smoke billowed from the rear as it churned its way through the water. Only one of the lifting fans was rotating but it was enough to compensate for the water in the hull. Var fought to keep the vessel in a straight line and headed for the yacht ahead.

The passengers on board the yacht were desperately trying to raise the sail, whilst others aboard did what they could with the boat's oars. Despite its deteriorated condition the chasing metal vessel was rapidly catching its prey. Var could see through the broken cabin glass that they were only a couple lengths away, when the engine suddenly spluttered and died. The boat lurched forward in the water as the fan keeping it above the waves spun to a stop.

Var thumped and kicked the controls in a wishful attempt to restart the seablade. He looked up as he heard a high pitched whine coming from the front of the boat. A deafening hiss of compressed air echoed out and Var could see the boat's harpoon arc out in front of them.

The huge barbed metal missile hit its target, plummeting through the cabin of the wooden yacht and exploding splinters in all directions. Gero picked up the end of the rope attached to it and started to pull hand over hand. The seablade was now taking on water and listing badly. The crew of the harpooned boat tried to row against the giant in a mammoth tug of war.

They were managing to hold the Magta warrior until Var appeared over the side of the boat and dispatched two of the rowers.

"You can take your chances in the sea" hollered Var. "Or you can take your chances with him once he draws you in." Var pointed towards Gero who was now hauling the vessel in at speed. The Dumonii civilians needed no further encouragement and leapt from the captured boat.

The wooden yacht bumped gently against the metal plates of the partly submerged seablade, and Gero jumped aboard. Air bubbles erupted from deep in the hull of the ruined vessel as it gave out its last breath. It slowly disappeared into the depths.

"Let's go fishing" smiled the giant.

Chapter 4 - Ascension Gate

"The men are ready" reported the Captain.

"Good" replied the Helmsman. "This is finally what we have been waiting for Petr. At long last the riddles of the old crone are starting to make sense. This is the city that I am destined to rule."

"If the people are anything to go by it would seem that this place has seen better days" said Petr.

"All civilisations have their highs and lows. This is a case of poor leadership that is all. We know how to survive and prosper in the bleakest of conditions. We will transform this city and its people." Toll-Son-Ray noticed his Captain's attention wandering. "I know what occupies your thoughts my friend. Rest assured when I am installed on the throne of this city, you make take as many men as your require and pursue your own agenda. I can see the flames of anger in your eyes, but we must focus on the task at hand."

"You know me well my Lord. I am at your service as always. How do you intend to break these defences? This fortress seems more formidable than that of the giants" asked Petr.

"That is true. The last thing I want to do is destroy these fine battlements, they are the prize my friend. There are however more ways than simple brute force to open a gateway. The state of these people as you so acutely observed is the key to the first of these doors. The scouts report that the ramparts are manned by civilians. It seems that the ruler of this city has no care for his people. We can use that to our advantage. It is time to get things underway."

The Helmsman lowered the visor on his helm and spurred his mount forward. The captain of the Red Prime followed close on his heels. They made their way through the ordered lines of cavalry and foot troops. The huge towers of the Last Bastion soared upwards before them.

A nervous defender inadvertently loosed an arrow. The Helmsman remained still as he watched the path of the projectile. The arrow clattered harmlessly to the stonework some way behind the Merthurian forces. The Helmsman turned to Petr and smiled.

"This may be easier than I thought" he whispered. The leader urged his Shektar forward once again and stood alone in front of his forces.

"Hear me people of this great city! I am Toll-Son-Ray. I lead the army you see before you. We find ourselves here by chance. By some twist of fate we have been transported to your city. We have had to re-evaluate our future and now we all must make difficult decisions. Your choice is this. You can open the gates and embrace me as a leader and my men as brothers or you can hide behind your walls. We wish you no harm but if the gate does not open, know this. We will breach these walls and when we do there will be no blessing. If the doorway remains closed to me you are condemning every man, woman and child within this fortress to death."

Toll-Son-Ray pulled on the reigns of his mount and the enormous animal reared into the air. As it thumped back down onto the cobbles it roared its impatience.

"I can promise you one thing as your leader. Fairness. Your own ruler has left you here to face us. He has left you here to die. Ask yourselves this. Is that fair? I know how difficult your lives have been. You starve whilst watching friends and family die of disease. How has your leader helped you? We come from a desolate world, yet we prosper. This place is like a paradise to us. We can show you how to live, and live well. As you can see I lead my people by example. I stand here before you, as I would stand before any enemy. Where is your leader? Why does he cower behind his people? You have heard my terms. You have until Shu reaches its apex to give me an answer."

The Helmsman turned his beast and returned to the ranks of his army.

"That was a fine speech my Lord" whispered Petr.

"We will soon see" replied Toll-Son-Ray.

It was only a matter of moments before the grinding of gears could be heard within the defensive structure.

Chains rattled as the iron clad doors slowly began to open outwards. As the gap grew between the two colossal doors a tall thin man emerged and nervously made his way towards the Merthurian force. The Helmsman dismounted and made his way to greet the newcomer.

"My name is Soh-I. I am a Magister of the Dumonii. I speak on behalf the defenders of the Last Bastion and the Pinnacle. We would like to accept your gracious offer" said the man.

"You have made a wise decision Soh-I" answered Toll-Son-Ray.

"Before we relinquish control of the Pinnacle we would ask for a few concessions." The nerves were clearly showing in the Magister.

"Please continue" gestured the Helmsman.

"We would ask that all of the civilian population are allowed to leave and return to their homes in the lower city. We ask also that no clemency is shown to the Virtues once you finally confront them."

"Hah!" laughed Toll-Son-Ray. "A man after my own heart. Of course. The people may leave. We do not wish for any civilian casualties. All that I would ask is that perhaps you and maybe twenty of your social leaders would remain to advise us as we prepare for our assault. I assume that the 'Virtues' to which you refer are the incumbent rulers. Rest assured they will face my full fury."

The skinny man physically relaxed and breathed a deep breath of relief. He hurried back to the opening gateway and spoke with a huddled group of people.

News of the impasse solution quickly spread through the defenders and cheers and shouts echoed out around the fortress. Toll-Son-Ray climbed into the saddle of his mount and made his way unimpeded through the shadow of the huge defensive gate. The populace hurried past him making their way out from the Last Bastion. The metal portcullis of the Pinnacle Wall was being hauled upwards, and hundreds more nameless Dumonii spilled out from its mouth.

The grand exterior of the Hall of Justice dominated the inner court. Its massive supportive pillars dwarfing the myriad of statues and carvings covering the frontage. Gilt doors shone out from the obscured walkway.

"I am liking this place more by the moment" commented Toll-Son-Ray. Beside him the lean figure of Soh-I was panting as he tried to keep pace with the loping animal. Behind him were a straggling bunch of nervous individuals.

"My Lord. These are those that hold sway within our population. They will be happy to advise. We hope that we can prove useful to you." said Soh-I

"I am sure they will" grinned the Helmsman. "Tell me Magister. What lies beyond?"

"These are the Halls of Justice. They have been used as a makeshift hospital since the illness started to spread amongst us. Behind them is the Bridge of Lies. This leads across to the Ascension Gate. The Virtues will be holding that point. They refused entry to all nameless when your forces arrived."

"Interesting" pondered the Helmsman. "Why is it called the bridge of lies?"

"It is steeped in legend and lore. It is said that the Ascension gate is impregnable and that those standing before resort to any tale in order to be granted access."

"How appropriate" smiled Toll-Son-Ray. He turned to face Soh-I.

"What do you mean by nameless?" he asked.

"It is our culture" started the Magister. "Those who hold any position in our society have an associated name that defines their status. Those who serve in the armed forces or those in positions of senior administration qualify. The rest of us remain un-named."

"Barbaric" stated the Helmsman. "I would ask one final favour from you Soh-I."

"Of course my Lord, how can I serve?"

"I would ask you to cross the Bridge of Lies and relay my terms of surrender to your Virtues. Do you think you are up to that task?" asked Toll-Son-Ray. Buoyed by pride the Magister rolled his shoulders back and bowed his head slightly.

"It would be my honour" he replied.

Toll-Son-Ray and Petr looked out from the rear gate of the Halls of Justice. The deep man-made scar between them and the towering Ascension gate stretched right across the island almost severing it in two. The thin bridge seemed completely out of proportion to the fortress beyond, like some forgotten thread clinging to a loom. They watched the figure of Soh-I stride out along the Bridge of Lies.

"Do you actually think this will work?" asked Petr.

"Of course not. A starving populace is one thing, but a society based around military prowess will not succumb to threats. It shows a fine strategic mind in placing the civilians in the outer defences. They could have slowed us down maybe even inflected serious casualties. Their fighting force would still be fresh. I admire this Virtue" replied Toll-Son-Ray.

The lone figure of the Magister neared the mighty gateway. No words could be heard from this distance, but the single arrow that was fired from the battlements could be clearly seen jutting from his chest as he buckled and fell to floor.

"I guess we have our answer" smiled the Helmsman.

"What now?" asked Petr. "That is a serious proposition. We would lose many men attempting a full frontal assault. I cannot see another way around."

"As I said before my friend there is more than one way to unlock a door. We have time on our side. Their supplies of food and water will eventually run dry. They will need to come to us or starve to death. Even if they do not they will be weakened. We will help speed their decision along. It is time they appreciated how serious I am."

The Helmsman walked to speak with the civilian leaders.

"As you can see, dialogue seems to be out of the question. So we must find another way to break their will" said Toll-Son-Ray. "How many sick and diseased are in the hospital below?"

"Two hundred, maybe more" replied one man. The Helmsman returned to his Captain and summoned his other charges to gather.

"The two trebuchets mounted at the front of this building, bring them here and aim them towards the citadel. Petr get your men to escort all of the sick and injured below and bring them up here to the roof. They will be our ammunition."

Petr swallowed. "Are we to kill them first?" he asked.

"Only if they resist. I think the screams will add to

the occasion. We will start with the group of leaders over there."

Petr placed a hand on the Helmsman's arm.

"Are you sure you want to tread this path my Lord?" he asked quietly.

"No fear and no remorse my friend. Pity is for the weak. Get it done."

*

Vas emerged from the small trapdoor. The heavy hatch slammed as it crashed backwards into the rock face. The Emperor cursed at the sound. As he emerged from the confined tunnel he realised that the sound of the breaking waves on the rocks below would have drowned out any noise he could have made.

There was no other way into the Outer Ward other than across the Bridge of Lies but the Emperor knew every rock and crag of the island and after crawling through a narrow tunnel had come out on the cliff below the Royal Palace. It was an old mining tunnel and had not been used in ages.

As the sea air cleansed his nostrils he wiped the grime from his armour. He looked up at the near vertical rock face. He flexed his fingers and rotated his shoulders trying to loosen his muscles. He felt the rock for a hand hold and with his toes wedged into a deep crevice he started to haul himself upwards. The wind whipped around him as he climbed steadily, taking care to keep three points of contact with rock. Beads of sweat ran down his cheeks, as his arm and leg muscles burned from exertion. Despite his vast strength he was not a natural climber. For once his muscle bulk played against him.

Tufts of grass and small ground hugging plants signalled his ascent was almost over. The rock around the base of the fortress walls was rarely traversed and provided a haven for wildlife. The incessant buzz of insects filled his ears as he reached down to strap the climbing spikes around his boots. Thin metal blades protruded a short way out from his toe. He then slid each hand into similar contraptions. The smooth stone of the citadel was near impossible to climb. The master masons that constructed the great walls cemented each block together with amazing skill. Leaving only a fraction of space between each block. It was not enough for a finger hold but the sharp metal spikes could find purchase. The elements had eroded the mortar over the revolutions and Vas chipped away exacting a route up the great wall.

The whole climb had taken far longer than he had anticipated, but to his advantage the light now faded as he crested the battlements. He made his way unnoticed across the parapet and dropped down into the Royal compound. He discarded his climbing equipment and crouched low behind an outlying building. His original plan was to lie low until just past midnight before trying to enter the keep. With the amount of Reavers and

Missionrai milling around he was sure he would be discovered long before then. As he looked out from his hiding place he witnessed the almost constant stream of soldiers moving in and out from the keep entrance. There were guards positioned on every tower and the beacon fires illuminated every corner of the courtyard. Stealth was never his preferred option.

"Plan B" he whispered to himself.

He placed both his war hammers and his dagger on the ground and walked directly out towards the flow of soldiers. His nonchalant gait carried him as far as the main gate until finally one guard recognised the intruder. Vas raised his arms above his head.

"I am unarmed. I have news of the invading army and I wish to speak with the Virtues" stated the Emperor. By now his actions had attracted the attentions of all around. Whispers ricocheted through the ranks and a cautious Missionrai approached Vas with his sword drawn.

"You can check if you like" said the Emperor. The man circled Vas looking for signs of weapons. If the Emperor had decided to hide a blade the lack of conviction from the guard would have kept it secreted.

"Wait here. I will inform the Virtues" said the Missionrai.

"What is your name?" asked Vas.

"Don-Te" replied the man.

"Well Don-Te. I am sure you know who I am, and while I know you must be cautious I have no intention of waiting here. You may bind my wrists if you feel it necessary. Then you will escort me directly to the Virtues. Else I will kill you where you stand."

Don-Te signalled to his fellow guard who shortly returned with a length of rope. The Missionrai tied Vas's hands tightly behind his back. Though he could not see the soldier Vas felt the man's hands tremble as he completed the knot. Feeling more secure and wanting to re-affirm his authority, Don-Te shoved the Emperor forward.

"Let's go" he ordered.

Vas surveyed the halls as he was led through the keep. Apart from the lack of cleaning the familiar surroundings had remained unchanged. He noticed that his banner and that of his father had been removed. He smiled at the pettiness of the rogue Virtues. They finally approached the double doors of the war chamber.

"You will wait here" demanded the Missionrai. He met the Emperor's gaze. Vas stared unblinking at the soldier. Don-Te turned and made to open the door.

"Hurry up" added Vas.

The Missionrai glared back at the Emperor before entering the brightly lit room. Vas looked at the remaining guard.

"Do you have family?" asked the Emperor politely.

"Yes" said the Reaver in a gruff voice.

"You may want to return to them" said the Emperor firmly.

"I'm not scared of you. You are the nameless. You are a disgrace to the Dumonii Emperors" declared the soldier.

"And you are a fool" growled Vas as he slipped one of his hands free from his bonds. Before the guard had a chance to draw his weapon Vas clamped his hand around the man's throat. His vice like grip crushed the hapless Reaver's windpipe. Vas lowered the strangled guard to the floor. He removed the dead guard's sword. It was a crude weapon. Vas tossed the sword onto the body of the soldier. He looked around the decorated walls of the keep. On every wall were weapons of every description. Vas removed a large round shield. It had a mythical beast breathing fire embossed upon its surface. He slid the imperial aegis onto his arm. His eyes searched along the array of weapons before locking onto an appropriate object.

He returned to stand before the closed doors and smiled as he heard the shouts coming from within. Footsteps increased in volume and he tensed. As the merest sliver of light cracked through the doors Vas rammed his blade through the gap. He had chosen a Dargyll sword. It was a simple ancient weapon. The length of a normal sword but its blade was four times the width. The weapon ended in a diagonal point and the hilt of the sword was surrounded by filigree cage, protecting the hand. The weight of the sword was substantial and Vas's biceps bulged as he ripped the weapon free from the chest of Don-Te.

He stepped over the cleaved body of the Missionrai and turned to shut the doors. A throwing knife thumped into the door beside his head as he used his old bindings to secure the door handles. He turned to face the fractious Virtues.

"Gentlemen" intoned the Emperor.

"How dare you!" blurted Frey-Aka.

"Calm yourself!" shouted the Virtue of Air. The four Principles and six guards fanned out in front of the two Virtues. "To what do we owe this pleasure?" asked Alu-Aka.

"Oh I think you know" stated the Emperor. The Virtue of Air laughed.

"So your plan was to break into our chamber and kill us all single handed. Or have you brought some of your furred friends to help you?" suggested the Virtue. It was the Emperor's turn to laugh.

"I need no help in dispatching two cowards and their nursemaids" said Vas calmly. "It saddens me to see how far the city has fallen. The people starve and you sit here ignorant to their suffering. There is no glory in ruling if there is no one left to rule."

"You would lecture me about rule!" shouted Alu-Aka. "It is your blindness that has wrought this situation. Your lack of adherence to our revered ways, your disdain for your father and all that he stood for. It is your head that the people crave."

"The world ends and you look to the past for salvation. I thought the screams of the dying that bombarded your walls this rotation would have woken you from your stupor. But even when death howls at your threshold you cannot see what you have become."

"I knew the hellion at our door were of your making" sneered the Virtue.

"Yes I brought them here. But I have no allegiance to them. The man who knocks at your door is the epitome of evil. You should be giving thanks that I will end your miserable existence before he steps foot inside this palace. The rest of your men will not be so lucky. It is your greed that now brings about the collapse of the once great Dumonii civilisation."

Vas lurched forward swiping downwards with the immense blade. The momentum of the weighty sword sliced through the nearest soldier's arm and continued to sever his leg just above the knee. Spinning and crouching Vas unleashed his next attack. The vicious sword disembowelling another victim.

The Emperor brought his shield up blocking a thrust from a pike. He pressed forward slamming the shield into the wielder's face. Shattered teeth and blood gushed from the man's mouth. A sword point chinked from Vas's shoulder plate and another found a gap in his side. Ignoring the sting of pain Vas turned bringing the Dargyll weapon over his head. The blow sundered the guard's helm in twain. The severed part of the helmet clanged onto the floor disgorging a slab of flesh.

Blocking once again, Vas rammed the blade forwards impaling two guards at the same time. The second fell away holding the gaping wound in his stomach. The Emperor smashed his shield against the Reaver stuck on his sword pulling back at the same moment.

A morning star wisped over the edge of his shield and the spiked ball drew blood as it raked down his chin. Snarling, the Emperor dropped low swinging the sword in a far-reaching arc. The wide blade sliced through the ankle of a Principle. Vas used the falling man as a stepping stone and vaulted onto the solid marble table. He jumped, somersaulting over the next advancing Principle. He landed and reversed his blade, ramming it into the administrator's back.

He looked across the room and saw the Virtues running for the rear door. Two principles were left barring his way. He slid his arm free from the shield handles and grabbing it by the edge launched it towards the men. One was quick enough to avoid the projectile. He ducked as the spinning disc slammed into the neck of his comrade. Before he had a chance to turn the Emperor's blade tore his head from his body. Vas kicked the severed head towards the fleeing Virtues.

Frey-Aka turned as the skull skittered into the back of his legs. Panic filled his lungs.

"Hurry!" he yelled. Alu-Aka fumbled with the ring of keys and at last found the right one. It turned in the lock and the two men bundled through. The Virtue of Air was up first and sprinted down the long corridor. Frey-Aka's overweight frame hampered his escape and he turned onto his back to see the Emperor fill the doorway.

"Please, no.." His plea ended abruptly as Vas thrust his blade into the Virtue's chest hewing his heart in two. The Emperor pulled the heavy sword out, the metal blade rasping against the dead Virtue's breastplate.

The Emperor caught up with Alu-Aka as he again tried to decipher the correct key for the next locked door. He turned dropping the keys. The Virtue of Air gasped as the massive blade ripped through his stomach and pinned him to the wooden door. He grabbed the blade trying to stop his weight from sagging further onto the sword's edge. Blood bubbled from his mouth. Vas grabbed the Virtue by the chin and looked into the dying man's eyes.

"You lose" said Vas.

*

The small sailing vessel had struggled to make it through the choppy water. The boat was now anchored off the Southern tip of the Island of Hope. Var and Gero were busy bailing out water that had been taken onboard during their short trip. Bronsur and Gav-Sem were both asleep in the cabin. Gero's crude attempts at patching the shattered timber kept out the light but water now sloshed around beneath the sleeping pair.

The main problem was the creature that was also fast asleep on the prow of the yacht. It had taken some considerable effort to get Hotay onto the boat in the first place. The constantly yawing sensation had initially upset the huge beast, but after he had cleared a suitable area he had slept for most of the journey. Even the waves that broke over him didn't seem to disturb him from his primal dreams.

The extra weight meant that the boat sat very low in the water. Var was exhausted from the continual and repetitive exercise. As his eyes adjusted to the evening darkness he sat back satisfied that the job was done. In the lea of the island the sea was much calmer and the gentle rocking of the boat soon had all occupants deep in slumber.

*

The Emperor picked up the keys and thumbed through them. He found the master key and opened the door. Alu-Aka remained pinned to the door. He squeezed through the reduced opening. Removing his sword he ran down the long corridor inside the outer wall. He remembered these passageways from his younger life when he and his brother used to dare each other at Rogan's Leap. He headed there now. He opened the last door and stepped out into the cold night air. The chill wind rapidly cooled his overheated body and he shivered in anticipation. He made his way to the edge of the southernmost tower know as Rogan's Leap. It was so named according to legend by the first person who had jumped from it and survived.

The tower soared way above the waves below. It had been used to bring supplies directly into the Outer Ward. A long unused hoist stretched out over the battlements, and way below the seabed had been dredged allowing larger ships to berth without grounding. It had been the perfect place to prove your manhood as an adolescent.

Vas peered over the edge. It looked much higher than he remembered and his stomach flipped at the thought of jumping. He strained his eyes in the darkness as he scanned the sea below. He saw a large white object. On further scrutiny he could see the boat that bobbed beneath what he now knew was Var's Shektar.

He took one step back and then before his mind could convince him of his folly he launched himself off the tower. Several moments later he hit the water. The impact stung his feet and sent waves of pain up through his legs. He spread his arms attempting to slow his descent, and then kicked hard for the surface. As he broke through he breathed in sharply, his lungs screaming for air.

His armour was hampering his efforts to swim towards the boat. He had left his hammers behind and had no intention of shedding his imperial armour. A heavy arm reached up and grabbed the wooden rail of the boat. The Emperor unceremoniously hauled himself into the vessel. He thumped onto the deck bringing yet more water into the yacht. He looked around and despite his noisy entrance all the occupants remained fast asleep. Vas smiled to himself and shook his head. He made his way to the stern and started to haul in the anchor.

*

In the rotations that followed the gruesome bombardment of the Ascension gate things got steadily worse for the defending Dumonii. With no sign of the invading force all anger was focussed inwards. The news that both Virtues and their Principles had been murdered triggered rumours and rivalry. Various factions started to form in the ranks of the Reavers and petty squabbles over food or whose turn on guard duty got out of hand and lives were lost. The Missionrai tried to keep control but without a leading figurehead their authority dissipated.

Meanwhile the remnants of the Merthurian horde waited patiently, planning for the inevitable. Only three rotations after they had arrived unexpectedly in the city of Sagen-Ita, Toll-Son-Ray accepted the unconditional surrender from the Missionrai For-Te.

Later that afternoon in a hurried ceremony the Merthurian Helmsman was crowned as the new Emperor. Toll-Son-Ray sat proudly on the grand throne. Bathed in reflected light from the crystal dais, he sat as an equal to all of the carved ancient heroes that lined the God Crypt.

One man approached him, bowed in respect and then climbed the steps up to the throne.

"Ah my friend. I know why you are here" laughed the new Emperor. "My word is as stone. Take what men and resources you require. May the gods smile upon your hunt."

"Thank you my Lord" replied Petr.

Chapter 5 - Pursuit

The Red Prime Captain backhanded the man for the second time. Blood trickled from the corner of his mouth.

"This is the last time I will ask you" warned Petr.

The old man wiped blood onto his sleeve and spat the rest onto the floor.

"I have no idea what you are talking about" he complained.

Petr's attention was distracted as one of his men came bursting into the shack.

"Captain."

"What is it Quinn?" asked Petr.

"Tracks. We have found a set of tracks. A single Shektar and several other boot prints. It has to be them" reported the section leader. Petr returned his focus to his captive.

"It seems you do know something old man. Let me explain how this is going to go. First I will cut each toe from your feet. Then I will start with your fingers. If you are still not talking and are still conscious I will pluck out each of your eyes."

A whimper came from the corner of the room. Petr raced

towards the sound and hurled the wooden bed across the room. Cowering in the corner was a young girl.

"You leave her alone!" growled the old man.

Petr grabbed hold of her by the hair and hoisted her from the floor.

"Well maybe you will talk to save this child?" asked Petr. The girl squirmed under his grip.

"Leave her be. I will tell you what you want to know. He'll kill you anyway." All of the fight drained from the old man. Petr released the girl and she ran to the man. He hugged her tight and glared up at the Red Prime Captain.

"He was here. Three rotations ago" said the old man.

"And where was he going?" asked Petr slowly drawing his sword.

"You'll kill us both, so what's the point?"

"Grandfather, please tell him" cried the girl.

"Listen to the youngster old man. You have my word I will spare you both, but only if you stop wasting my time. Have no doubt I will let my men mutilate your granddaughter if you try to thwart me further" warned Petr.

"He is heading to the mountain village of Keihin-

Hab" sighed the old man.

"And why would that be?" inquired Petr.

"He believes an old friend lives there. He is in need of his help. That is all I know, I swear."

Petr looked deep into the eyes of the man.

"At last you tell me the truth. I assume they are travelling on foot. How long would it take to reach this village?"

"Four maybe five rotations" said the man.

Petr moved to the edge of the door and looked out at the beached yacht on the shore. He turned to confront the frightened pair once more.

"How long by sea?" asked Petr. The old man fell silent. "How long old man!" bellowed the Captain.

"Two rotations at most. It would depend on the vessel" he conceded.

Petr smiled.

"Quinn. Go and talk to our helpful Dumonii skipper, tell him to prepare for a sea crossing. I will be along shortly" commanded Petr.

"Yes Captain." Quinn cast one last glance at the old man and his granddaughter before leaving.

Petr sheathed his sword. He picked up the dirty jerkin he had removed from the old man earlier. He threw it towards the duo. The old man looked confused.

"You're not going to kill us?" he asked in disbelief.

"The threat of violence is far more effective than the act itself. We all fear what we do not know, including the threat of pain. Once we experience it, the fear subsides and with it any leverage. I have killed many in my time, but I am no animal. I am glad I was convincing."

Petr turned to walk from the small shelter. With his back to the pair the young girl jumped up and lunged at the Captain. Her small rusty knife sunk into his side just above his hip. He grimaced at the red hot shock to his system. Unthinking he drew his sword and turned plunging it into the girl's chest. The old man screamed and ran towards him. Allowing the dead girl to fall to the floor, he repeated the stabbing action skewering the old man through the solar plexus. Life quickly faded from the old man and he collapsed onto the body of his granddaughter.

Petr clasped at the wound in his side.

"It did not have to be this way" He whispered. He knew that his words were a plea for his own soul. He also knew that forgiveness would never be forthcoming.

He walked solemnly from the shack and made his way to the small rowing boat. His men cast nervous glances between each other but none dared speak, they could sense his inner rage. Quinn shuffled forward in the boat. He flicked a fleeting look at the two rowers. They both shook their heads. Quinn decided to ignore them.

"May I ask a question Captain?" proffered the section leader. Petr remained mute, but Quinn took this as a positive response. "The man we seek. Who is he?"

Petr continued to stare blankly at the deck. There was an uncomfortable silence.

"He is my fate" said Petr suddenly, breaking the atmosphere. "Long ago when I consulted with the Morrg she told me that I would meet a warrior with only one leg. He would be the one who would kill me. When the ocean woman told me about her betrothed and his artificial leg, I knew he was the one. I had intended to keep her close, hoping she would lure him to me. That was only partly successful. I do not believe my fate was set from birth. I will take control of my own destiny. I will find him and I will kill him."

*

The Emperor was waiting for the rest of them at a fork in the road.

"We have a choice of routes" he explained. "We can go that way." He pointed left towards the Caucasus Mountains. "Or we can continue along the coast and then follow the River of Determination. That will take us through Vallis Pass. It is a much easier route but it is perhaps two maybe three rotations longer."

"How long since we first arrived here?" asked Var.

"Three rotations" replied Vas.

"Then we should take the quickest route" suggested Var. "We have no idea what is happening back on Gebshu. The sooner we can return the better."

"That is assuming we can return my friend. Please do not get your hopes up. This is a long shot" explained the Emperor.

"I have made it this far on hope, I have no intention of stopping now" smiled Var.

"It will be dark before we cross the mountains. Do we intend to camp up there?" asked Gav-Sem with an uncharacteristic nervousness.

"What are your concerns?" asked the Emperor.

The burly Dominator seemed reluctant to speak his mind. The Emperor smiled with understanding.

"You mean the Nookoo, don't you" said Vas.

"That would be it" admitted Gav-Sem.

"And what exactly is the Nookoo?" inquired Vas.

"It is just local lore. The Nookoo is the supposed guardian of the mountains. People believe it to be a six legged animal that preys on the unwary traveller. I heard the stories when I was a boy, and have heard cases of missing people and mutilated corpses, but the mountains are a dangerous place. I have crossed this mountain range many times and never seen anything. It is just a night-time story to scare the young."

"Well it has me on edge" said Var.

"We still have a choice of routes" offered the Emperor.

"Pah!" spat Gero as he took the left fork towards the mountains.

The climb up to the snow topped mountains was not that difficult - just a hard slog. The route was narrow and at times unclear due to the lack of footfall. Var struggled as he led Hotay. The huge animal often had to detour around narrow gaps. This was alien country to the Shektar and it laboured on the steep climb. Bronsur had ridden him since they had left the sinking yacht behind. Hotay had been uncomfortable at first with carrying a different rider, but the attention Bronsur lavished upon him soon had the white beast compliant.

The light began to fade and to further hamper visibility a thick fog descended on the group. The Emperor called a halt as they came to a large rock overhang. They worked quickly piling stones at either side of the makeshift shelter. The wind started to pick up and much to their annoyance was blowing directly into the overhang. They continued working into the night building a rock barricade. Satisfied with their work they all clambered inside. Hotay settled across the entrance completing the windbreak.

Although the wind had caused further work it had also cleared the fog. The occasional star blinked in the darkness. Var moved his arm around Bronsur's shoulders and pulled their blanket up. He stared out into the blackness and watched mesmerised as a single snow flake drifted into view. It was soon followed by more and within moments the bare rock was slowly being covered with a white carpet. Var continued to watch the building snowfall until he eventually fell asleep.

Var started from his dreams, woken abruptly by a low growl. It was Hotay. He had moved from the entrance and stood growling at the darkness, his hackles raised.

"Wake up!" yelled Var.

The others were already waking.

"What is it?" asked Gero.

"It's Hotay, he has sensed something out there" said Var.

The four men drew their weapons and stood shoulder to shoulder at the entrance to their shelter. Var moved towards his Shektar. He placed a placating hand on Hotay's neck and smoothed the agitated animal.

"What is it boy? What can you see?" asked Var.

He stared into the distance, scanning each and every rock outline looking for movement in the gloom. A blood curdling howl split the silence and echoed off the mountain passes. Hotay roared back a challenge and before Var could attempt to stop him he vaulted into the night.

"Hotay! No!" screamed Var. He made to follow his bonded animal but Gero's large hand clamped down on his shoulder.

"That's not a good idea Var" he said quietly. They group tensed in hushed concentration.

Demonic howls rang out all around, as if they were entirely surrounded by the unknown protagonist. Var's hands tightened around the hilts of his swords, looking for the merest whisper of threat. Nothing happened. They waited unmoving.

"There!" shouted Gero.

A massive shape flitted between the rocky outcrops in the foreground. They couldn't make it out, but something was slowly creeping towards them. Gero hefted his axe onto his shoulder ready for combat. A low rumble came from the darkness. Var lowered his swords and walked towards it. As he moved forward the blurred creature came into view. It was Hotay. He had blood dripping from his fangs and his front legs had red matted stains scattered all over them.

The Shektar snorted as Var cradled his huge head.

"Good boy" Var whispered into the animal's ear. "I bet whatever it was out there wasn't expecting you."

"He's hurt" called Bronsur.

On his hind leg were four deep gashes and fresh blood was also oozing from a puncture wound on the back of his neck.

"He'll be okay Bron. I just hope he has killed whatever it was out there" said Var.

"The Nookoo" said Gav-Sem.

"Perhaps we should forego sleep this night. It may be wise to continue onwards, we can reach Keihin-Hab at first light" suggested Vas.

The nervous party continued to trek through the night but had no further encounters or mishaps. As the morning light started to wake the countryside, their destination could be clearly seen in the foothills. Like the larger towns of Sunem-Por and Ment-Por that they had travelled through, it looked deserted.

"Is this where your friend lives?" asked Var.

"It is the last place I heard of him, and he is not exactly my friend" replied the Emperor.

"How so?" inquired Var.

"He was my brother's and my mentor when we were younger. My father employed him to teach us the ways of war" explained Vas.

"I guess you were an unruly student then" smiled Var.

"On the contrary. I was his finest protégé. He was a master of arms and I learnt much from him. Unfortunately at the age of fourteen I bested him in a display of unarmed combat. My father then asked him to leave his employ, satisfied that he had nothing left that he could teach me. My father made many mistakes, but that was one of his best."

"I am sure your old teacher won't hold what happened in the past against you" soothed Var.

"You have yet to meet him" said Vas raising his eyebrows.

"True" replied Var. "I guess we also have to find him first."

"Oh that will be easy. You see the hut set away from the rest, with the tall wall and fence around it. That will be it" said the Emperor.

Shu was high in the sky as they made their way into the village. Unlike the larger towns that had been devoid of life, this small village bustled with activity. The local inhabitants made no attempt to hide their amazement of the newcomers. They stopped and stared as the giant Gero and the blood-soaked Hotay stomped through. As they made it to the outlying hut of Vas's mentor they had attracted quite a crowd. The Emperor made his way to the entrance and rapped on the door. The door eased open and an ageing face appeared.

"Yes?" said the man.

"Souk-Te. It is me, Vas. I have need of your assistance" said the Emperor.

The old man looked Vas up and down.

"No thanks" he said slamming the door.

Vas turned and shrugged his shoulders.

"Perhaps he does blame you" shouted Var.

Suddenly the door opened once more.

"You're still here" said Souk-Te. Vas looked puzzled. "Who are they?" asked the old mentor.

"They are my friends. We are in need of your help" explained Vas.

"The white thing will have to wait outside" said Souk-Te and he turned back into his home. Vas beckoned for the rest to join him. The hut was sparse. What was there, was clean and neatly organised. The old man had returned to sit in a single rocking chair. He took a long pipe from his pocket and after packing in more leaves he took a long draw on the object.

"Do come in. You'll have to forgive the lack of chairs. I do not have any visitors."

The group squeezed in and sat on the floor like expectant pupils.

"Do you remember me?" asked Vas.

"Of course I do. I am old not senile, stupid boy" muttered Souk-Te. Gero cast a cheeky smile at Var.

"I don't know what you're smirking about. It is not like you can hide away is it?" berated Souk-Te. Suitably admonished Gero stared at the floor. Var moved his arm slowly across nudging the giant's leg.

"So, what has brought you here young Vas. Has your father come to his senses? Does he want me to complete your training?" asked Souk-Te.

"My father is dead" replied Vas.

"My condolences" said Souk-Te.

"It was me that killed him" said Vas.

"I never did like him. So that must mean you are the Emperor now then?" asked the old man.

"Does news ever reach this village?" asked Vas.

"It does. But no-one ever talks to me so I may be a

little out of touch. Besides no news means no bad news. You are wearing imperial armour, and although it looks like you are carrying a little extra weight, you certainly look like an Emperor. You must have remembered a thing or two that I taught you. What about that impetuous brother of yours, where is he?"

Vas lowered his eyes.

"You didn't kill him as well did you?" asked the shocked mentor.

"No, but he is no longer with us" said Vas quietly.

Var fidgeted uncomfortably.

"A lot has happened since my father asked you to leave all those revolutions ago. I am not the same person you taught in those innocent times" said Vas.

"You are still the same person I knew all that time ago. You may have experienced what life has to offer, but how else do you think you earn all these wrinkles. They are my badges of achievement. Tell me young Vas what do you need?" ask Souk-Te.

"Believe it or not we are trying to return to the ocean planet Gebshu. Unfortunately during the civil war between myself and the Virtues all of the shimmer gates were destroyed. We were hoping you might know of one that survived, perhaps at the temple of Maroc-Mor?"

"Destroyed you say. Not good. I have to say that I

do not know of any. The priests at the temple are a law unto themselves, so there is a chance their gate is intact. There is an eremite brother I used to know there. If there are secrets to be kept, he would be the keeper. His name is Rap-I. You should seek him out if he is still breathing. Do not let his scrambled mind fool you, he is a canny individual."

At that moment a young boy crashed into the room.

"Uncle, Uncle!"

"What is it boy?" asked Souk-Te.

"More strangers. They are making their way up from the river" replied the boy.

"What do they look like?" asked Vas.

"They are warriors, like you sir, but they have painted faces."

Vas cast a look of concern at the others.

"It looks like we have brought ruin upon you my old friend. They are here for us. They will tear this village apart looking for us" explained Vas.

"Then you best waste no more time here. Head out the back. You can skirt around the village and out behind them. Make your way to Maroc-Mor. I hope you find what you are searching for young Vas" said Souk-Te.

"I cannot leave you here to fight alone" pleaded

Vas.

"You forget your place young noble. Emperor you may be, but my liege you are not. I gave up taking orders when I left Sagen-Ita. I am too old to change. Besides have you forgotten my prowess on the battlefield. I will buy you the time you need. Now hurry. I will argue no further" said Souk-Te.

"My Lord. If you will it, I will remain also" said Gav-Sem. "It has been my honour to serve."

Vas embraced the Dominator.

"The honour is mine" said the Emperor.

As the party ran from the back of the village the old warrior donned his weathered breastplate and slid his arms into his battered vambraces. He lifted his old sword from its hallowed resting place above the hearth and slung it over his shoulder. He turned to the Dominator.

"How sharp is that sabre of yours?" he inquired.

"It's good enough to shave with, if that's what you mean" replied Gav-Sem.

"Good, head down into the town, and hide in one of the houses. I will bring them here. When you have a chance come at them from behind. Hamstring as many as you can."

The Dominator nodded his understanding and left the hut.

Souk-Te strode from his meagre dwelling and walked to the end of his pathway. He stood with hands on hips awaiting the newcomers. The inhabitants of the village wasted no time in directing the fierce looking warriors towards the old man.

"I am not sure you have brought enough men" provoked Souk-Te.

"And you are?" asked Petr.

"I am that which blocks your way" replied Souk-Te.

"I don't have time for games old man" growled the Red Prime Captain.

"And I don't play games young fool."

In one fleeting moment Souk-Te drew his bastard sword and held it aloft. He muttered a few indecipherable words before settling into a fighting stance.

"So be it" replied Petr.

The first warrior to attack the old man suddenly realised what this unassuming character must have spent his whole life doing. Souk-Te allowed the soldier to thrust before he darted out his own sword lying it flat on top of the attacking blade. He rotated his wrist with a quick flick. The movement sent the soldier's blade spinning into the air. As the shocked warrior watched his sword in disbelief, Souk-Te lanced his blade clean through his neck severing the spine. He returned to his original fighting stance.

"Next" he beckoned.

At the same time Gav-Sem ran from a nearby hut. The column of soldiers all stood with their backs to him watching the play ahead unfold. Sword drawn he swiped at the rear of the knees of the nearest soldiers. The sharp curved tip of his sabre ripping open tendons. He had incapacitated six men before the Red Prime reacted. His brave charge was ended swiftly as sword after sword pierced his torso. Gav-Sem fell face first into the mud. Several more jabs entered his back, the soldiers making sure of their kill.

The aging mentor had dispatched two more warriors that had attempted to confront him. One warrior, unseen, had climbed the fence of Souk-Te's garden and crept quietly up behind the defiant man. He drew his sword and was about to stick the old man, when Souk-Te turned and his blade lashed out across the soldier's face. The man screamed in agony as the sword tip split his eye socket.

In that brief moment with the old man's back presented to him, Petr stepped forward and rammed his spear into Souk-Te. The tip of the weapon split through the front of the old man's breastplate. Souk-Te staggered forward dropping his sword. Petr released the spear and watched as his enemy fell to his knees.

Coughing up blood Vas's former tutor reached out his hand in front of him. It was as if he was expecting someone to help him up.

"Even in darkness there is colour" muttered Souk-Te as his last breath deserted him.

"Find them!" Petr yelled impatiently at his men.

*

The temple of Maroc-Mor although not the grandest of the Dumonii temples was no less impressive due to the position in which it had been constructed. It was built on three stacks of rock which ended a ridge running down from Mount Illera. The main temple was on the end of these rock columns. It was separated by some distance from the next two smaller conclaves. The three parts of the temple had originally been connected by precarious rope bridges but these had long since been replaced by ornate arched versions. A man made pillar now stood between the end Temple and its precursor. The distance was too great to be covered in a single span. The closest section between the temple and the artificial pillar consisted of a long drawbridge.

Its remote location had left it unchanged and unchallenged and the architecture reflected times long past. Unlike the square and hexagonal towers found over the rest of Son-Gebshu, Maroc-Mor boasted softer curves and round bastions. Multicoloured pennants flew from the tall circular towers and hundreds of small birds weaved between them like some arcane cloud.

The temple of Maroc-Mor had stood guard at the convergence of the two rivers at its feet for hundreds of revolutions. If ever there was a place disengaged from the politics of the capital then this was it.

As Var reached the summit he turned to ensure Bronsur and Hotay had made the climb. Bronsur had recovered enough strength and had insisted on leading what was fast becoming her Shektar up the hill. The difficult climb was so steep in places she doubted she would have made it in Hotay's saddle as he scrambled up the path.

"Hurry!" yelled Var.

Not far behind were forty or more soldiers led by Petr, and they were closing fast. The others were waiting by the first bridge. Gero stood ready with his mighty axe drawn.

"I'll hold them here" said the giant.

"We all make it back or none of us do" yelled Var. "We leave no-one else behind."

The group ran along the bridge and into the first and smallest part of the temple. It, like so much of the kingdom looked deserted. As they exited out onto the second bridge Var stopped and looked at the stone doorway.

"There must be a portcullis or something. We could slow them down" suggested Var.

"There is no time. We must get to the temple and lift the drawbridge" replied Vas. As he spoke he saw the emerging Red Prime make their way across the first bridge. Running at full tilt Var was the last one through the second temple enclosure. His leg was sore and it was starting to hamper his speed. As he made it out onto the final span, he baulked at the view. It had not been that apparent from the valley floor but now, stood on the thin walkway, the colossal height of the bridge made him shake. This, coupled with the lack of any edge barriers, made one wrong step fatal.

He finally made it into Maroc-Mor where Gero and Vas had already started to lift the long drawbridge. Gear after gear had been woven into its mechanism making it possible for two men to easily lift the cantilevered weight. That ease came at a price. Speed. Gero span the handle as fast as he could and it hardly seemed to move the drawbridge. They continued at pace and Var looked out along the inward route. Petr was out of the second temple and heading for the rising bridge. He had no intention of slowing and as he neared the widening gap he leapt.

One hand grabbed the lip and the other plunged a dagger into the wooden planks. He hauled himself over the edge and slid down the bridge. He landed in a cloud of dust and stood ready.

"I think you may have left something behind" indicated Var. Petr looked over his shoulder. His retinue were not filled with the same fervour as their captain and had not risked the jump. They stood helpless as the drawbridge sealed them off from their leader.

"It matters not" replied Petr.

"I am sure it doesn't" said Var. "But this must be the first time you have ever been outnumbered." Gero, Vas and Bronsur mounted on Hotay filed in behind the Doyen.

Petr was an accomplished warrior. He had fought fearlessly and faced death many times in battle. Always he had in the back of his mind the words of the Morrg. "You will meet your demise at the hands of a one-legged warrior". Until now that had never occurred and knowing this prophecy had given him superhuman strength and resolve. He had felt invincible. That security now vanished, as before him stood a man that could kill him and indeed was foretold to do so. For the first time since his youth Petr tasted fear. He spat his distaste on the ground.

"You'll face me alone?" asked the Red Prime Captain.

"It makes no difference to me. You will die here. Although I did make a promise" said Var.

Var slid his blades together and sparks danced along the edges. Petr drew his sword and lashed upwards towards Var's chin. Stepping back Var blocked the riposte and swung low with his razor sharp Magta blade. Petr anticipated the move, jumped and landed on the sword bringing his knee up into Var's face at the same time. Var fell backwards releasing the grip on one of his weapons.

He recovered quickly and clambered to his feet as Petr attacked again. The Red Prime Captain went for the killing blow. A direct stab towards the neck. Var stepped into the attack blocking the strike. He span along the blade and thundered a punch into Petr's side. The blow would have winded most but Petr yelled in agonising pain as the infected wound he had suffered three rotations ago, opened afresh. He staggered backwards trying to block out the pain.

Var attacked with renewed vigour, raining down a flurry of strikes, each one taking a notch out of Petr's sword. With his adversary on the back foot Var slammed a repeated punch into his side. This time Petr dropped his sword and fell to the floor. He tried to reach for his weapon but the keen edge of Var's mattock lopped off his hand. Blood spurted out on the flagstones as Petr screamed in pain. Var knelt over the prone Captain and with his hands firmly clamped on either side of Petr's head he snapped his neck.

Var retrieved his sword as Bronsur ran to hug him.

"He can't hurt us now" he soothed.

"Well fought, well fought" came a voice from the background. A small grey haired man came towards them clapping his hands together. "Haven't had that much excitement since..." He looked upwards pondering. "Well we simply haven't had that much excitement ever!" he exclaimed.

"Are you alone old man?" asked the Emperor.

"Oh no of course not. There are hundreds of us here. Silly man" he replied. Vas looked around the desolate temple. Apart from numerous birds there were no other signs of life.

"You must be Rap-l" said the Emperor. "I am a friend of Souk-Te."

"Souk-Te you say. Cannot be. He has no friends" replied Rap-l.

"I was in his charge many revolutions ago. He said you may be able to help us" explained Vas.

"Help you. Maybe I can. What is it you need?" asked Rap-l.

"We need to find a working portal. We wish to travel to Gebshu" said Vas.

"The portals have all gone. By royal decree. I would not dare disobey the word of the Emperor"

"Souk-Te said that you didn't care for the rule of central government. He said that you might know of somewhere?" probed Vas.

"Did he now? No wonder he lived alone. I am sorry he was mistaken. It looks like you have travelled far to be here. I can only apologise for your disappointment. Come, I can show you the old gateway. It still remains in pieces" said Rap-l.

"Can it be mended?" asked Gero.

"My you are tall. Mended. No. The Lexan is smashed. Only my forefathers had that knowledge. Come anyway. You look tired. I have food and drink. It has been a while since I had visitors."

They followed the stooped priest into a small refectory. They moved out the pews and sat at the table. Var allowed his head to thump into the table. Rap-l moved to and from the kitchen bringing wine, fruit and fresh bread. He sat opposite the Emperor. Vas picked up the bread. It was soft, still fresh, as though it had been baked that rotation. He tore off the end of the loaf and breathed in the pleasurable smell. As he placed the loaf back on the table he noticed the symbol baked in dough on the top.

"This is Devhn bread?" said Vas. "Where did you get this?"

"Umm. I have it delivered" offered Rap-l apologetically.

"It is at least two rotations to Devhn-Por. This bread is fresh, and I would know this mark anywhere" quizzed the Emperor.

"Undone by bread!" exclaimed Rap-l.

Var lifted his head from the table.

"What exactly does that mean?" asked Var.

"It means that our friend Rap-l has a way of travelling to Devhn-Por and back again fast enough to keep the bread fresh." said the Emperor.

"Perhaps he is a champion athlete?" smiled Var understanding the importance.

"Yes that's it" said Rap-l "I have trained all my life. I am very fast."

"We do not care that it exists old man, we simply need your help in using it to return home" explained Vas.

"Okay, Okay. Yes there is a portal. But it is only a small one." Rap-l tried to look innocent. Realising he was fooling no-one he clapped his hands. Several men appeared from the kitchens and stood waiting for orders.

"Where did they come from? I thought you said you were alone?" asked Gero.

"Not alone. Hundreds I said. Hundreds. Go and prepare the gateway. Find the Servillisor with the deep baritone voice. We will need his chords." The men hurried away and Rap-l beamed a vacant smile at his bemused visitors. "Follow me."

"I need to get Hotay" said Bronsur.

Rap-l turned.

"That animal. You want it to go through as well? I don't think it will fit. We may have to shave it."

They followed the priest down several flights of stairs. Bronsur and Var had to pull and push Hotay down the narrow corridors until they eventually emerged into a small domed chamber. It was unlike any other gateway they had seen. The Lexan stone was built into the walls and curved upward meeting at the apex. It resembled the construction of the sea pods.

"So to what gate do you travel on Gebshu?" asked Rap-l. He picked up an intricate golden globe. It was a scale model of the ocean planet and had red jewels embedded over its surface. "Which one?" continued the priest tapping the sphere.

"There are no gateways we are aware of. We constructed a new one, that is how we got here" said Var.

"New. No. That won't do. It must be marked on this map."

"We need to get to the Pillars of Itna. Can you take us there?" asked Var.

"It is not a carriage my young friend. The shimmer portals can take you anywhere with the right frequency. It is not the travelling but the arriving that is the problem. Unless you travel from gate to gate there is no way of discerning how you will arrive" said Rap-l.

"What do you mean?" asked the Emperor.

"I can target a location, and most of the time I get

that right. But without a gate to focus on you may arrive in the clouds, beneath the ocean or worse still inside something. It is too dangerous. I cannot do it" mumbled the priest.

"We will take our chances Rap-l. Do your best. Whatever happens we will not be back to complain" suggested the Emperor.

"True. Yes that is true. Then try I will."

More servillisors and servants entered the room and took their places at each of the Lexan uprights. They began to chant. The rhythmic humming increased in volume and the stone behind each man began to glow. The atmosphere flicked and static built up in the confined space. Rap-l fiddled with the golden globe and gestured to one of the servants. The man increased his pitch. As he did the middle of the chamber imploded and the gateway fizzed into life. The centre of the room seemed to swallow the light and reflect it at the same time, as the portal pulsed in and out like a beating heart.

"Who's first?" asked Rap-l.

Without hesitation Gero stepped forward. He disappeared into the miasma. Vas followed him and then after some persuasion Bronsur went next. Var pushed Hotay towards the flexing vortex and finally he shimmered out of sight.

"Thank you" said Var.

"Maybe" said Rap-l as Var walked out into the void.

Chapter 6 - The Pillars of Itna

The cold rush of freezing air against his skin was the first sense Var became aware of. The second was the sensation of falling. As the shimmer portal closed he saw the pack ice rushing up towards him. He landed heavily. His good leg took the main force of the impact as his artificial appendage buckled underneath him. He hadn't fallen that far, but far enough to be painful. He lay face down on the frozen surface. Despite the cold and the pain there was something re-assuring about the familiar harsh environment.

He looked up to see Gero, Vas and Bronsur standing a short distance away. They look worried. He turned to see Hotay next to him, still in shock from the journey. Then he heard the sound. A loud crack. The weight of Hotay crashing onto the ice had considerably weakened it. Jagged lines shot out in all directions from Var and his Shektar.

Normally the ice would have been too thick, but the summer was approaching and they were near the equator. The sea ice was rapidly retreating and thinning.

Var watched in horror as the web of fractures grew. He slowly lifted himself up, the slippery surface groaned and popped at every flex of his muscles. Hotay moved towards him and the ice suddenly buckled.

"No Hotay! Stay still boy" shouted Var.

Still confused by recent events the huge animal remained still, looking to its master for guidance.

"Good boy" calmed Var.

He looked up at the others who were also having to make a retreat back from the breaking ice.

"It's thicker over here. Quickly make your way to us" hollered Gero.

Var looked back down at the cloudy brittle surface. His blood froze as he glimpsed a black shadow twist beneath the ice.

"Oh no" he whispered, fearing that even his voice would cause the ice to split.

He looked all around. The dark shapes now flitted in all directions. He stepped forward gingerly. As he did a black blur thumped up beneath the ice. Var panicked and ran. Each step sent out a bone chilling crack reverberating through the ice. He was only a short distance from his friends when the surface gave way. Seeing Var run, Hotay had followed. The weight of the colossal animal had stressed the delicate surface and the Shektar crashed through into the sea. A hole opened up and rapidly widened.

Var disappeared under the freezing water. He kicked his legs hard, fighting the mental shock of the intense cold. He trod water frantically trying to climb onto the broken ice. As soon as he obtained a handhold the ice would shatter dumping him back into the water. Fear welled in his throat as he felt the smooth lash of a Kekken tail brush next to his leg.

Behind him Hotay was having the same trouble. The animal was a good swimmer but as he tried to pull himself from the water he only succeeding in widening the fissure. The great beast roared in pain as long black claws raked at its flesh. The furred animal fought back kicking in desperation and ducking beneath the surface trying to bite at its tormentors. Hotay crashed back through the floating ice debris. His long curved teeth had impaled one of the Kekken. It flailed and squirmed as the Shektar shook its head violently. The sea creature tore in half spilling its guts into the ocean.

Undeterred by the increasing number of writhing creatures tearing and ripping at its skin, Hotay defiantly made his way towards Var. As he neared he submerged. Var felt a solid mass hit his legs. Hotay swam upwards and used the massive muscles in his neck to launch Var from the water. The Doyen was catapulted from the sea and landed, skidding across the ice.

He scrambled to his feet and ran to the edge of the hole. Bronsur held him back.

"You can't help him" she said.

Var watched with tears streaming down his face as Hotay

bravely tried to fight his way towards him. The Kekken swarmed over the great animal and eventually succumbing to his myriad of wounds, and the overwhelming number of creatures, Hotay sank beneath the bloody water.

"No!" screamed Var in frustration.

At that moment a shiny black creature leapt from the water. It skidded to a halt before them, hissing its hatred. Before Var could react the butterfly axe of Gero ripped the Kekken in two. Another two animals crawled from the break in the ice. Var drew his swords.

"We need to make it to the island Var, before the ice gives out altogether" pleaded Bronsur.

More and more Kekken were climbing out from the gash in the pack ice.

"I am going to kill them all" swore Var.

"Not now" warned the Emperor. "Bronsur is correct. The island is still some distance, we must make it there while we still can. This is their territory. We will fight them when we have the advantage. Come, we must move."

Reluctantly Var joined the others as they ran towards the island chain of Korem. The ice was becoming dangerously thin and another passing moon would have seen the mass break-up of the remaining Southern Ocean sea ice. As the group made their way up across the rocky shore of the first island Var stopped to look back for the first time. There was no sign of the sea creatures. Although they could survive out of the water, they could not spend any length of time away from it.

Bronsur sat on the rock next to her promised. She hugged him tightly. Gero and Vas continued on to the island leaving the couple to mourn in peace.

The Korem Archipelago consisted of many small islands in a long chain running from the ancient ruins of Manitoba in the North to the Pillars of Itna in the South. One of the main sea currents, the Haf Stream ran along the island and then out across the Great Ocean. This body of water was continually in motion and always the last part of the ocean to freeze in winter. Now in the slightly warmer clime it had broken free of the pack ice and large peaks and troughs rampaged on either side of the island chain.

The landscape showed the intrusive signs of habitation. Most of the pine trees had been felled as the Dumonii, Magta and Ocean peoples had moved across the islands. The destruction, albeit necessary, scarred the once picturesque panorama.

"It looks like they have left us a trail" said Gero as he kicked the cold remnants of a fire pit.

The first few islands were only separated by narrow stretches of water. The shallow divides were still frozen and the party hurried across them on the constant look out for the ever present sea creatures. Two of the larger islands were connected by a rocky isthmus. As they clambered over the rocks the water below them teemed with Kekken, like some primordial soup.

The gap between the end of the larger landmass and the next island was considerable. They could now see why most of the timber had been harvested. A long wooden bridge extended out over the gap. It was weighted down by large boulders at either end. As they crossed the makeshift construction Var looked down between the planks. Thousands of Kekken swam in the fast moving current. He felt sick.

As they reached the other side voices rang out and a crowd of people swarmed down the hillside. Mort and Mido bounced into Var hugging him and then kissing Bronsur on the cheek.

"You made it Var!" exclaimed Mort.

"Told you he would" tormented Mido.

The exuberant twins lifted Var's mood. He watched as Lothair and Hanelore grasped forearms with Gero and as the Emperor acknowledged his waiting entourage of Dominators and the Virtue of Water.

"We had started to doubt your return" said Hanelore.

"You are not the only one" smiled Var. "I take it the

bridge is your handiwork?"

"It is a joint effort. The Emperor's people have some interesting ideas when it comes to engineering and construction. I thought I was too old to learn, but they have proven me wrong. It is good to see you safe young Var. I take it your Shektar did not survive the trip back?"

Var shook his head.

"We have all sacrificed much to this world. Let us hope we are nearing the end of this struggle. We have only one more divide to cross to reach the Pillars, but there would have been little point without you. We will now move this bridge across the island and use it again on the other side" explained the old giant.

"No way back then" said Var.

"I have always preferred 'forwards' as a direction" laughed Hanelore.

As they walked towards the main encampment, and much to Var's surprise, the initial segregation he had observed had been blurred at the edges. Magta sat in conversation with Dumonii and that of his own people. He smiled at the integration. As the masses noticed the returning warriors, a cheer rang out around the camp. The chorus continued and grew in volume and passion. Embarrassed, Var and the others acknowledged the welcome. Any victory, however small, was something to hold onto.

The ramshackle barracks had been constructed from all and any materials at hand. Most were fabric tents or wooden lean-tos made from fir tree branches. Groups of them were clustered around central cooking fires. In spite of the cold conditions and the loss of home comforts, life continued. Children played in the muddy main thoroughfare seemingly unaware of the black ring of death that surrounded them.

As the light faded Var warmed himself next to one of the fires. A lithe woman approached him.

"It is good to see you" she said.

"And you too Lin" replied Var. "This is my betrothed, Bronsur."

The two women shook hands.

"Please, join us" suggested Var.

"Can I ask what happened? I saw you charge into them, and then everything vanished" said Lin.

"It was my fault" conceded Bronsur. "He came to rescue me."

"And so he should have" replied Lin.

Var started to tell the story of their adventures on Son-Gebshu. Within moments he had a crowd of people all pushing to get close enough to hear his tale. With some extra flourishes Var regaled the events that had unfolded on the moon to a captivated audience. As he completed his story and told them of Hotay's brave end, even a few of the surly men had to quickly hide their emotions.

"He saved your life" said Lin.

Var smiled, but he couldn't hide his sadness. Lin noticed and changed the subject.

"There is one last crossing until we reach the Pillars of Itna" she said.

"Yes, Hanelore had mentioned it. We will move the bridge in the morning" replied Var, grateful for the switch in topic.

"There is a problem. Although we will start from a high vantage point on this island, the bridge will only reach the rocky shore opposite. There is a good chance that the Kekken will attack before we can reach the higher ground. Each time I have ventured even close to the water's edge, they seem to appear. I hate those things, they give me the shivers."

"We will find a way" said Var simply.

"I know we will" replied Lin. "There is a large cave set into the cliff below one of the pillars. If I was going to build a secret gateway that would be my first choice. When we make it across we should look there."

"Let's hope they are still at home" smiled Var.

"And if they're not?" asked Bronsur.

"Then this will be an awkward summer vacation" said Var.

*

It was mid morning before the Doyen woke. Hanelore's gruff tones stirred him from his deep slumber. The events of the past moons had taken their toll. Var wiped his eyes and stretched as he shed the thick fur blanket that had kept him warm during the night.

"Good, you're awake at last" said Hanelore.

"Good morning to you too" replied Var.

The old giant ignored his sarcasm.

"We have been discussing the bridge. Whatever we do, it is likely that the Kekken will attack at some point. We are trying to weigh the risks of our approaches" explained Hanelore.

"What have you come up with so far?" asked Var.

"Well, we just have the one idea" confessed the giant.

"Which is what? Run for it?" laughed Var.

The giant didn't share his amusement.

"Really? That's the best we can come up with?"

asked Var.

"Our Devastators and the Emperor's men would cross first and then form a defensive corridor from the end of the bridge to the high ground. The rest of the population would then run the gauntlet. There would be casualties" said Hanelore.

"What about when we make it across - how do we intend to get everyone down the cliff and into the cave? Supposing that's where it is" asked Var.

"One problem at a time young Var. I was thinking..." the giant's voice trailed off. Var recognised the look on the giant's face.

"What? What is it you want me to do?" queried Var.

"I was thinking about the link you have with the sea creatures. You have communicated with them in the past. Perhaps you can do so again, at least to find out their intentions" said Hanelore.

"You want me to just wade into the sea and ask them?" replied Var.

"Of course not" said Gero, joining the conversation. "We are going fishing." He flipped a strange looking arrow over in his hands.

"Well in that case, let me get my boots on" laughed Var.

The small group made their way out across the rocky shoreline. It didn't take long before they had piqued the interest of the sea creatures. Gero leapt from one boulder to another as he made his way to the water's edge. Several Kekken had already surfaced and were making their way cautiously towards the bounding giant.

Var waited some distance back accompanied by the Emperor, Lin and a handful of Dominators. Lin notched the arrow Gero had been holding to her bow. She stepped to one side making sure her feet were clear of the cord piled on the floor. As Gero now hurried back he was closely followed by eight black shapes. Lin pulled the bow string to her lips and loosed the arrow.

The shaft flew through the air, the twine coiling out behind it. She had aimed slightly higher than with a normal arrow, allowing for the added weight of the attached line. As the arrow neared its target it dropped and punched a hole through the shoulder of one of the chasing Kekken. As the barb erupted out of the animal's back, four thin spines sprang out. The creature hissed at the pain and tried to pull the shaft from its body. The splayed spines meant that would be impossible without ripping its shoulder to pieces.

Before it could understand what was happening the Dominators had pulled on the cord sending the animal flying face first into the rocks. They continued to pull as fast as they could dragging the harpooned Kekken up the beach. The other animals stopped their pursuit. Gero turned and removed his cloak. He threw it over the struggling animal. Using a length of rope from around his neck he wrapped it around the prone creature.

"Gero!" shouted Var.

The giant looked up to see one of the other Kekken had continued its pursuit. It launched itself, claws tensed, at the burly giant. Gero slammed his fist into the face of the animal sending it flying backwards. He stooped down picking up an enormous boulder. Lifting it above his head he walked to the injured beast and dropped the stone. Var heard the squelch from his position up the beach and cringed. Gero cursed as he pulled several of the Kekken's needle teeth from his knuckles. He returned to the struggling covered animal and let fly with a vicious kick. He hauled the dangerous bundle from the beach and made his way back to the others.

"Make sure you hold it tightly" warned Var. Gero, and the Dominators had the creature pinned to the floor with its arms and talons held firmly at its side. "I hope this works" said Var as he reached out and grabbed the creature around the wrists. It had been a while since he had mind linked with the Kekken but the dizzy feeling hit him as soon as he touched the captive animal.

[Kill you] came the unhindered thought into Var's mind.

[Believe me the feeling is mutual] returned Var.

[Kill you all]

[Why? Why do you want to kill us all? You helped me once. It was your brothers that told me of the prophecy. They told me of my destiny. They even sent me here. They wanted me to open the gateway of the Gods. They believed that only they could save us. How has that changed?]

[The hive was diseased. Our memories not clear. The disease cured now. The chosen must not open gate. Gods will be angered. They will destroy us. You must not open gate. Our memory is clear now.]

[If I do not open the gate you will all die eventually. This world is ending. You and your brothers must sense it? How long has it been since you swam in warm waters? Will you not let me try? If there is a supreme being he would surely care for all of the beings in this world. I understand your fear but I have come this far. I am not turning back now]

[You must not open the gate. Must not change cycle.]

[What cycle?]

[Cycle of death and life. Gods create world this way. We cannot break what they set in motion. Death is part of cycle. If all breathers of air must die then this is God's will. We must stop you.]

[What if you cannot?]

[Then Gods finish what we start]

Var broke the link and sat back fatigued on the wet sand.

"What did it say?" asked Gero.

"Looks like we'll be running the gauntlet after all" said Var.

The Emperor drew his knife and swiftly slit the creature's throat. It twitched and spasmed before its arms went limp.

*

The warriors amassed on the headland of the island. Behind them the civilians had packed their belongings and were ready for the trial ahead. They had left many of their possessions behind as anything that would slow them down could not be taken.

The Magta Forged caste rolled the bridge into place. It was supported on stripped tree lengths. They had several thick ropes attached to one end. They manoeuvred the enormous span into place stretching precariously out over the ocean. As the weight slowly moved past the fulcrum the giants started to take the strain. The rope was looped up over two massive 'A' frames. The height of the frames allowed them to slowly move the bridge into place. As it neared its position on the far side, black shapes started to appear at the water's edge. The bridge slammed down onto the rocks. It bounced once before settling, but the Magta and Dumonii warriors were already racing across.

The Kekken had started to emerge from the ocean in large numbers as they realised what was unfolding. The first giants across the bridge slammed into the few animals that had climbed to the bridge. Their blades sliced the black flesh asunder. They filed in as ordered forming a shield wall on either side. As they continued to pour in they formed a living causeway from the end of the bridge to grassy land above the beach. With the warriors still forming and filling in any gaps Bronsur led the rest of the people across.

The Kekken crashed against the defensive line like a black tide. Razor sharp talons rasping and searching for unprotected flesh. Slick heads, full of needle sharp white teeth, biting and tearing at anything in their way. The armoured warriors held firm stabbing and jabbing furiously, trying to keep their bodies behind their shields. At the point where the bridge landed the warriors were four deep. They had to contend with the largest amount of animals. As the dead bodies started to pile up the Kekken used them to try and jump over the shield line. The rear lines held spears and pikes anchored on the ground and impaled any that attempted a breach.

Notwithstanding their formidable armour and sound strategy the defenders were gradually losing men. An over extended arm jabbing outwards was seized upon and the warrior was torn from the ranks. His screams pierced the air as he was ripped to pieces under the sea of Kekken.

Bronsur had made it across and was hurrying those behind her to safety on the island. The line of people still stretched back across the bridge. The creatures had started to leap from the water and were now crawling over the bridge dragging those not quick enough into the churning water. Kekken at the other end of the bridge were tearing and clawing at the supporting ropes. As they snapped, the bridge teetered before the animals pushed the far end into the ocean. The creatures surged along the buoyant platform devouring everything in their path. As the last few survivors made it in to the defensive corridor the warriors closed in, sealing the way to safety. They hurriedly fought a retreat back up the beach. Civilians had joined the defence and rained down arrow after arrow into the limitless Kekken.

As Var reached the hillside he looked out over the carnage. The beach was entirely covered by the creatures. Thousands upon thousands of them. A black plague. There were more still in the ocean desperate to join the turmoil. He looked away as the Kekken infestation finally swallowed the few beleaguered warriors and civilians that had not made it to safety.

As they moved further up into the island, the creatures halted. They turned and within moments had returned to the ocean, leaving behind a grisly sea of dead and dying. The alliance had lost forty to fifty soldiers. Hundreds of ordinary people also lay dead, floating in the shallow water. The loss of the bridge had cost them dearly. The Kekken dead, like those living, were uncountable.

The sombre mood of the camp continued into the night as they tended wounds and sought to regain a semblance of normality. Guards had been posted around the top of the island. Unlikely as it was for them to attack, they were not taking any chances. The zeal with which the Kekken had fought had frightened even the most seasoned warriors.

*

As the morning light warmed the ground Var and Gero stood peering over the cliff edge. It was a considerable drop to the rocky shore below. There was a narrow path that wound its way down the cliff, but both men decided they did not want to reveal a quick access point to the sea creatures. They had secured a rope at the top of the cliff and were debating who should make the climb down to examine the cave.

"It will hold your weight. It held the weight of the bridge" argued Var.

"That is your opinion. It would make more sense if you went as I can pull you up easier. I'd like to see you pull me up!" exclaimed Gero.

Var shrugged, trying to think quickly of another excuse. As the two men held each other's gaze Lin ran between them and picked up the end of the rope. She dived headlong off the cliff.

"Make sure you have the other end" she said as she disappeared over the edge.

The two men scrambled to grab the rope as it uncoiled. It went taught as Lin swung beneath them and into the recess of the cave.

"Are you okay?" called Var.

"Of course" came the reply.

"She's not right" whispered Gero.

"I heard that" came the voice from below.

Var laughed.

"What can you see?" asked Var.

"This is it. There is some sort of door here. It is massive. It has markings all over it but they are hard to make out. It looks like it has been submerged for most of its life as its encrusted with arthropods. There are remnants of steps but most of them have been eroded by the waves" replied Lin.

"Well my friend, we have reached the end of our journey. We now just have to find a way of getting everyone down the cliff face and hold off the sea beasts while you work out how to open the gateway. Then once we get inside, if we can, we have no idea what we will find. So we could end up in an empty cave trapped by thousands of Kekken who have one single purpose - to kill us" posed Gero.

"I agree. It's not the best idea I have ever had" said Var.

"Hey gentlemen! I hate to interrupt but is there any chance you can pull me up. I have some unwanted company" shouted Lin.

Var looked over the edge and beneath the suspended Lin were the Kekken. They had poured out from the ocean and were jumping into the air trying to snag the dangling woman. Gero heaved on the rope and in moments Var was helping her over the edge.

"They didn't take long to appear" said Var.

"This is going to be harder than we thought" said Gero.

"Not necessarily" said Hanelore appearing over his son's shoulder.

"You have an idea?" asked Var.

"Well not me exactly. The Dumonii replicators have suggested something. I think it will work but we need time to prepare it. I will need more pine trees and also we will need to collect the Benzl from every lantern. Oh and as many clay pots that remain" instructed Hanelore.

Under the old giant's explicit guidance the people of the alliance spent the day at their given tasks. Var and Gero joined the majority in the small pine woodland on the island. Instead of chopping the trees down as they had expected, they had to drill holes in the tree trunks and collect the sap. Hanelore had explained this as 'tapping' a tree.

Gradually the various groups came together with their completed materials. Hanelore and a handful of Replicators had spent the time building a small catapult. They had positioned it at the edge of the cliff above the cave entrance. The pots had been lined up and the sticky mixture of Benzl and tree sap were carefully mixed into them.

Once again the warriors and civilians alike were prepared to move. Var headed the column along with the Emperor and Hanelore. Gero, Lothair and Lin remained to arm the catapult. The two giant brothers loaded the machine and after quickly winding it back they fired the first pot into the air. The projectile sailed out over the beach and smashed as it hit the ocean. The giants worked frantically firing pot and after pot into the sea. With the last one flying overhead Var started to lead the people down the cliff path.

The contents of the clay missiles lay on the surface of the water and all across the rocks like a thick oil slick. As Var made it to the shingle, Lin sent out a flaming arrow. As it hit the ocean a wall of fire erupted into the sky. All around the Korem islands were underwater fields of Velpaynix. This was the seaweed that the ocean tribes used to breath beneath the waves. It produced oxygen in its natural state. These now fuelled the inferno that enveloped the ocean.

The Kekken leapt from the ocean trying to advance on the descending people. The sticky fiery liquid stuck to their skin and tried as they might by diving back into the water, they could not extinguish the fire. The Magta and Dumonii formed a defensive line across the entrance to the cave. They crouched behind their shield wall. This time they were not protecting themselves against the Kekken onslaught but against the heat wave that swept up from the flaming ocean. The sea creatures burned and the chill sound of their screams echoed from the cliffs. Those that made it onto the beach collapsed in agony as the flames devoured them.

Var ran towards the colossal doors. As he neared he could see the worn symbols and ancient text that covered them. As Lin had described, thousands of seasons of sea creatures had made their home over the surface. He removed the Emperor's seal from within his jerkin.

At his eye level was a depression. He removed his knife and started to chip the crustaceans away. With the keyhole suitably cleaned he turned to look at the Emperor.

"Well here goes" he said with a determined look.

"If this doesn't work, I doubt we will have time to make it back up" replied the Emperor.

Var followed the Emperor's gaze. The raging inferno was

losing its intensity. It wouldn't be long before it petered out and the black torrent of Kekken flooded into the mouth of the cave. Var placed the round seal into the gate. As soon as it touched the door, it retracted and a covering plate slid across the hole. Nothing happened at first. Then loud clicks and thumps sounded out and the gargantuan doors started to move.

Chapter 7 - Guardian

The doors slid back to each side, sloughing the encrusted sea life as they retracted into the cliff. As the outer door moved back an inner door sank into the floor. As it neared the ground the astounded Var watched as a further door lifted up into the rock ceiling. The stale air of a millennia spewed into their faces.

The inside of the cave was vast. The fading light from Shu only just penetrated it, the rest remained in utter darkness.

Var moved tentatively into the cave.

"We must all get inside" urged Hanelore. "The fire withers and dies."

Var and Hanelore remained by the open gateway as the people hurried inside. The Warriors retreated and formed up once more just inside the cave. Gero, Lothair and Lin dropped down from the rope above. Gero flicked the rope and it fell onto the shingle. He looped it around his arms as he walked towards the entrance. The shield wall opened to allow them inside. As the fire finally exhausted its fuel, the waiting hordes of Kekken started to rise from the ocean.

Var stared at the inside of the wall.

"There has to be a way to close the doors" he

shouted. They felt along the wall in a desperate hope to conceal themselves away from the rampaging sea creatures coming up the beach.

"I think this might be it" said Gero pointing upwards. Some way above his head was a large handle hanging down from the ceiling. "Why would they put it all the way up there" asked the giant. Var had already climbed onto his back and then onto his shoulders. With Gero holding his feet he reached up. He still could not reach it.

"Lin, quickly" he pleaded. The slim ocean woman clambered over the two men. Balancing precariously on Var's shoulders she jumped and clamped her hands around the handle. Her weight brought her and the contraption downwards. The inner door started to descend from the roof. The assembled peoples watched as the massive three part gateway sealed them away from the Kekken and away from Shu's fading light.

The alliance stood in total darkness as they listened to the outer doors slide across. The muffled sounds of scratching could be heard as the Kekken ripped their claws desperately trying to get inside, their hive mind burning with the thought of extinction.

In loud pops, large slabs of light appeared high up in the celing and continued to race back through the cave illuminating the immense interior.

"There are no flames" questioned Gero looking up

in amazement at the lights.

"Whatever they are the important thing is that they are working. After all this time they still work, that is incredible" remarked Var.

To the far side of the chamber was a tunnel leading down into the ground. After much discussion they decided a small scouting party would move into the complex. The rest would remain in the relative safety of the capacious cavern.

Var, Gero, Lothair, The Emperor and his Dominators walked cautiously into the long tunnel. Similar lights were placed at regular intervals in the walls as well as the roof. As they made their way downwards they could see a giant statue at the far end. Behind it was another door. As they neared the unusual sculpture suddenly a green light flashed within it.

The statue was three times the height of the Magta. It was constructed of metal. It stood on two legs, each shin protected with angular guards. In behind huge pistons supported the central section. This part had a large circular diaphragm set into it and above this what resembled a domed head. Protruding from each side were two huge arms. They were similarly linked by hydraulic rams and ended in metal fingered hands. On the left, what looked like a rusty fist guard, was angled next to the forearm. On the right arm in a similar position was a wheel. The circular device had curved blades surrounding the circumference. Running from over its back were two curved poles, that followed the contour of its body. Two enormous exhaust stacks stuck up from behind its shoulder plates. It had been painted once but the paint now had mostly flaked away. Every surface was rusted or displayed a corroded patina. The green light emanated from the centre of the head-like object.

The group were frozen to the spot as the object hummed and whirred and the green light intensified. Suddenly the machine moved. Its arms moved upwards and it rotated its hands. It then flexed its fingers. The hiss of the pistons was deafening. The group stared in amazed wonder. If not startled enough the machine then spoke.

Who wakes Solon? - Guardian of the Celestial Gate

Its voice rasped as if speaking was a considerable effort. The question echoed out along the tunnel. Var looked to the others for guidance. There was no answer on their shocked faces.

"I am Var-Son-Gednu, I come seeking an audience with the Gods" said the nervous Doyen.

Gods? - I am not familiar with that term. Do you mean the creators?

"Yes" replied Var. "The creators. We wish to speak with them."

Are you creator borne? # asked Solon.

Var looked at his comrades, who all nodded in unison.

"Yes I am" replied Var with fake confidence.

That is good. The test will confirm your validity.

With speed unnatural for a machine so large, it reached out a metal claw and grabbed Var. The pistons hissed and the fingers closed around him. Var struggled but the improvised cage held him tightly. Gero and the rest of the party drew their weapons. Var signalled to them to stand fast. Although he was trapped, the metal fingers were not hurting him. The Guardian lifted him from the floor.

Please place your hand on the sampling pad # instructed Solon.

Var looked at the metal configuration and on the inside of the hand was a distinct square pad. He reached forward placing his palm flat against it. As his skin made contact he felt a sharp prick on one of his fingers. He instinctively withdrew his hand. In doing so he smeared blood across the test pad. A small light flickered green. It flashed on and off and then turned red.

You are not creator borne. Termination protocol.

The Guardian threw Var across the tunnel. He smashed hard into the wall. The force of the impact knocking him out cold. His comrades reacted swiftly and attacked the mechanical monster. Lothair's hammer crashed against the shin plate. The blow sent reverberations up through his arms and succeeded in removing a few more flakes of paint.

Intruders. Safeguard mode initiated.

Row upon row of armoured plates now rose from the back of the Guardian. They moved on the rails that ran vertically on its body. They covered the diaphragm and its head. The green glow emanated from a small slit in the plating. The fist cover rotated forward covering the fingers of the left hand like a giant knuckle duster. Likewise the wheel on the right started to revolve and moved into place above the clenched fist of the machine.

Solon swung the spinning disc towards its aggressors. Lothair and Gero dived beneath it. The swing continued and spat chunks of rock into the corridor as it ground into the wall. The collision had not slowed the speed of the killing wheel.

"How do we kill this thing?" yelled Gero rolling to his feet. He hammered his axe against one of the leg pistons. Sparks flared but the weapon only left a shallow scratch. The Emperor and his Dominators had split up and were attacking from all directions. Ton-Sem had jumped and grabbed hold of the spiked fist guard. His arms burned as he tried to hold on. The Guardian moved forward and turned slightly. He thumped his fist up into the ceiling pulverising the Dominator instantly. Glass and rock rained down over the machine.

"Nothing seems to hurt it. We have to retreat" shouted Oma-Sem over the commotion.

"We cannot go back. It will kill the others. We have to find a way" said Gero.

The Emperor ducked beneath the armoured fist as the blow exploded rock shards into the tunnel. He sprinted beneath the behemoth and looked to its back for a way up. He jumped and grabbed a handhold hauling himself onto the Guardian's back. He climbed quickly looking for any weakness. He drew his sword from its sheath across his back. Wishing he still had his war hammers he rammed the blade in between the metal plates covering Solon's head. The sword tip reached its target but only succeeded in grazing the metal.

The huge metal hand reached up and before he could avoid them, the vice like fingers closed around his torso. Solon ripped the Emperor from his body and hurled him down the tunnel. He landed heavily, his face slapping hard into the stone floor. The impact broke his nose and blood streamed from his mouth.

Seeing their Emperor injured, the Dominators roared at the Guardian and renewed their attack. Ker-Sem jumped onto the front of the God machine and tried to stab in behind the metal plating at the pulsing diaphragm. To his surprise his sword punctured the vibrating surface. He continued in a frenzied rage repeatedly stabbing at the soft membrane. The hand of Solon closed around him and pulled the struggling Dominator free. Ker-Sem screamed as the fingers continued to crush him. His organs exploded as the hydraulic rams closed together. The Guardian dropped the mangled body onto the floor before hammering down once again.

The blow narrowly missed Lothair, and the giant staggered to one side. His unique maul remained un powered. There was no life-force for its vampiric head to steal. Tir-Sem dived into the Titan as the spinning wheel came arcing around. His actions saved Lothair, but the giant teeth of the disc eviscerated the brave Dominator.

Regaining his breath Gero unfurled the climbing rope wrapped around his shoulders.

"Grab the other end of this" he called to his brother. He threw the rope across the segmented foot of the Guardian and Lothair dived to grab it. Pulling it up he passed it to Oma-Sem who rolled behind the machine. Avoiding the devastating arms the assembled warriors managed to circle the legs of the machine three times. They moved back in unison encouraging the metal beast to follow them. As it did the rope pulled tight. They had hoped to topple the machine but its immense power simply snapped the three strands.

"I'll see you all in the depths" came the voice of the Emperor from behind them. He ran towards the Guardian. The spinning blade thundered into the ground as he vaulted high into the air. He landed on the motor of the disc and then jumped again onto the shoulder armour. He swung his leg to one side to avoid the grab from the other metal hand. As the arm pulled back for another snatch. He jumped onto the Guardian's carapace and clutched his sword hilt which was still sticking out between the plates. He pulled it free and with every fibre of his being thrust it towards Solon's head. The force of the blow shattered the tip of Vas's sword. Cursing he tried to withdraw the weapon. Before he could wrench it free he was caught in the Guardian's deathly clutch.

The metal rams sighed and began to crush the Emperor.

"Glory in death" spat the Emperor as his armour started to crack. The blood from his saliva ran down across the test pad. The red light flickered briefly before turning green. Solon suddenly stopped. The spinning disc slowly whirred to a stop and the fist guard rotated upward. The metal segments protecting its body slid back over its head splintering the rest of the Emperor's sword in the process. The Guardian lowered Vas to the floor.

Creator borne verified. Please state your command.

The Emperor bent over trying to refill his lungs with air. His laughter rang out through the tunnel. Gero, Lothair and the remaining Dominators stood in awed silence. They were woken from their exhausted trance by Var who was dusting rubble from his legs.

"What did I miss?" he said.

Solon stood motionless in front of them. They still weren't quite sure what had happened. Var limped across to join them.

"Did it say you were creator borne?" Var asked the Emperor.

"I believe it did" replied Vas. He turned to the Guardian. "What does creator borne mean?"

Derived from the creators. Blood descendant of the creators. Creator borne. # replied Solon.

"So my forefathers built this place?" asked the Emperor.

Your deduction is correct. # said the Guardian.

"Is it possible to speak with them?"

Yes that is a possibility

"Are they here?"

Negative. My program is to guard the entrance. You must travel to meet the creators. Do you require me to activate the Celestial Gate?

"Yes, I believe we do" said the Emperor firmly.

*

The remains of the Dominators' bodies were covered and

carried back to the main cavern. Var and the Emperor explained their encounter with Solon to the others. Much to their surprise the mechanical guardian appeared at the entrance to the tunnel. It explained that it would be some time before they could enter the gateway, as it required time to ignite. Understanding that Solon was created at the time of the first exodus, the assembled leaders had many questions.

Solon explained that when the first great cataclysm had befallen Gebshu the creators had decided they must use the shimmer portal technology to find a new, stable home. Even back then they understood that the planet had a finite life. The disappointment of discovering that the 'Gods' were in fact the ancient ancestors of Vas and the Dumonii was balanced as the story of their technological achievements was revealed. They had truly created a magnificent civilisation.

They had built several great gates that allowed travel to the moon of Son-Gebshu. They populated the moon with the cities that still stood all these revolutions later. A divided cabal of the Creators believed that even the moon would follow in the death throes of the ocean planet, so they devised the 'Celestial Gate'. Its purpose - to find a home elsewhere in the solar system. The success of their venture was unknown. Solon had been created to guard the gateway. His instructions only to allow access to those of the Dumonii royal bloodline. They had also devised another protector. The Kekken.

Knowing that the oceans would rise and submerge the gateway, they had used their advanced knowledge to contrive a creature that could survive beneath the waves. They gave these creatures the same ability to be able to recognise their descendants. They couldn't have known that these genetic experiments in nature would have become so successful and populate every ocean on the planet. It was easy to comprehend how their embedded memory had become confused over the vast time period. Although Var could not understand why they had recognised him as the 'Chosen'.

The Emperor had also seen how Var had been crushed by the recognition that the Prophecy had been flawed, thinking that his purpose in life was a lie. He had taken Var to one side.

"The prophecy is not flawed" said the Emperor.

"What do you mean? The Guardian recognised you as a descendant. It nearly killed me. Besides the key to open the door was yours in the first place. Although I do not understand how the Kekken thought I was the one" sighed Var.

"A long time ago my mother told me something. I did not want to believe it, I thought she said it out of spite and hatred. I put it far from my mind, but in my heart I have always known it to be true. The longer I have known you the more I have seen her attributes in your actions. I regret my last words to her."

"What are you talking about?" asked Var.

"You must have wondered why you are different to your brothers and the others of your kind?" replied the Emperor.

"Yes, my mother told me. She rescued me from Imercia when it was a prison colony. I was born to one of the nameless." said Var.

"Have you never wondered about your real mother?" asked the Emperor.

"Yes, I think about her from time to time, but as far back as I can remember Muadin has been my mother. She raised me as one of her own."

"That I can appreciate, but your real mother and mine are one and the same. You are my half brother Var" said the Emperor.

The ocean man stood motionless staring at Vas. He knew it was the truth. It explained everything. How the emotive Kekken could have identified him as creator borne but the binary mind of Solon did not compute his diluted blood. The relief that the last seasons of his life had not been a wild fantasy overwhelmed him.

"You are my brother?" Var stammered.

"I am. But that is not a term for public use" replied Vas.

"I understand" said Var.

With all of this new knowledge spinning inside his head, Var struggled to organise his thoughts. What did the future hold for them now? Var clung to the hope that the Gods still existed and that the Creators may have possibly found them. At the very least they had found a new home. A place where they could all start a new life. Vas couldn't help think about how far his birth line had fallen since their days in ascendance.

*

The people of the alliance followed the clanking Guardian through the tunnel and watched as the inner doors opened to reveal the Celestial Gate.

The light was blinding and the noise deafening. The completely spherical chamber had been excavated from the bedrock. It was gargantuan. Bigger even than the initial cavern. The entire temple of Ro-Mor could have been placed inside. Steps led down into the bottom half. Long lines of Lexan stone were expertly laid into the curved surface all traversing towards a central plinth. The top half was unlike any gate they had ever seen. It consisted of massive toroidal shapes decreasing in size as they formed a domed roof. They all glowed with a fluorescent white light, and vibrated with a subtlety that caused the newcomers to shiver.

"How can we be sure that the destination is safe? Have the creators ever returned?" asked Var.

Destination is unknown. The creators have not returned # replied Solon.

"Maybe a few of us should go through first, to make sure it is safe" suggested Var. He turned to the Guardian.

"Can a few of us travel and then come back for the others?" asked Var.

As many or as few may travel as you so command. I have no data to confirm your return # answered Solon.

"But if in theory, we did make it back?" said Var.

Then yes. The gate could be ignited once more. The estimated recharge time is twelve revolutions # stated Solon.

"Twelve revolutions! That's twelve seasons!" exclaimed Var.

"I believe this is an all or nothing event" said the Emperor. "Each of us should decide the position for our people. We have led them to this point, and so now we must have the courage of our convictions to lead them further. My mind is set. The Dumonii will follow in the footsteps of our forebears."

"This world has nothing left for us. The Magta will embrace the challenge" said Lothair.

"I guess this just leaves me then" said Var.

"Your judgement has not let us down so far my love" said Bronsur. "It is better that we meet our fate together. We know that whilst we remain here every eventuality ends in death. The smallest chance is better than no chance at all."

"Let us end this journey then. The people of the Ocean tribes stand ready" said Var.

"We all travel together Solon. Activate the gate when we are in position" instructed the Emperor.

As you command # replied Solon.

Tentatively the assembled crowd made their way down into the pulsating bowl. The cyclopean gateway could have swallowed them twice over. Light flared, and the Lexan reverberated, as sound waves fluctuated up and down the lengths of the unique stone. The pressure in the sphere increased threatening to shatter eardrums. The scared people held their heads as the pitch continued to rise.

In an instant the Celestial Gate convulsed and the remaining people of the ocean world of Gebshu vanished into the vacuum forever.

*

As the haze of the vortex subsided, Var's vision returned. He looked around nervously. The others had their weapons drawn, poised ready.

The gate at which they had arrived was mainly cloaked in darkness. Light streamed in from four small entrances at each point of the compass. Dust particles mixed with small buzzing insects were clearly highlighted in each of the openings. Var breathed deeply. The humid air was a mixture of relief and fear. Relief that he could breath. Fear that this place was unlike anything he had ever conceived. The hot atmosphere now washed over him like a wall of fire. His body temperature immediately started to rise. He removed his thick fur coat and let it fall to the ground.

"Feels like someone has left the fire on" said Gero.

The bright light and heat rushing in through the four doorways was a new experience but the most overwhelming sensation was the explosion of noise. The all encompassing roar was a chaotic mixture of squawks, screeches, hoots and chirps.

"Wait here with the others Bron. We'll see what awaits us outside" said Var.

He climbed the numerous steps towards the bright white exit. As they made their way upwards inside the gateway building the heat increased. Var stepped out into the hot and sticky atmosphere. He shielded his eyes from the intense light. As his pupils slowly adjusted to the contrast he stood open mouthed at the view before him.

He found himself standing atop a massive stepped

pyramid overlooking an ancient city. Beyond the collapsed city walls stretched dense jungle. The green canopy continued as far as he could see into the distance. The natural world had reclaimed most of the city with vines and creepers clinging to every surface. Trees and bushes erupted between the stone slabs pushing the once symmetrical masonry upwards into haphazard mounds.

The noise had emanated from the wildlife. Thousands of birds and insects sang out as they flew and scurried around, oblivious to the new alien arrivals.

"Look at this" cried Gero. Var hadn't even noticed that his giant friend had left, mesmerised as he was by the vista. He followed Gero along the pyramid, stepping over the roots and creepers that cradled the building. As they approached the worn corner stones, Var could see what Gero had been looking at. Out beyond the forest, standing like giant teeth were a long line of mountains. One had smoke wisping up high into the atmosphere, whilst another smouldered. It's grey cloud spreading out over its bare slopes. The chain of volcanoes stretched all the way across the horizon.

"Any ideas where we are?" asked Gero.

"Well it's not Gebshu, that's for sure" replied Var. "Let's find your father, he must have some idea. What about the rest? Do you think it is safe for them down there."

"We must remain on our guard" interrupted the

Emperor. "It looks harmless enough but our predecessors went to some considerable effort to build this place. I am sure they wouldn't have left it without good reason."

"That's assuming they are still alive" added Gero.

"Indeed" replied the Emperor. "There looks to be an inner wall surrounding this pyramid. We should repair the breaches in this as best we can. This would at least give us a solid defensive position, if it were needed. Until we can determine where we are and what we are dealing with, we should focus on security, and then food and water." Vas wiped the beads of sweat from his forehead. "Do you think this is what Gebshu once looked like?" he asked.

"We'll add that to the long list of questions for the creators" said Gero.

The wide-eyed people of the Magta, Dumonii and Ocean tribes spilled from the doorways in the ziggurat like busy lines of insects. They made their way into the compound surrounding the pyramid. Hands touched and smoothed the twisted bark of trees and delicate fronds of obscure looking plants as the people of Gebshu made their way into their new world. The novelty of the flora and fauna soon dissipated as all effort was focussed towards the crumbling stonework.

The vast majority of the defensive wall was intact. The architecture was similar to that of Sagen-Ita. The walls were wider at the bottom, tapering towards the top but still thick enough to allow three to four people to stand shoulder to shoulder. The outer sloped caps of the crenellations had mostly fallen into the undergrowth but the regimented archer positions remained, albeit worn by the elements. In two or three places huge trees had muscled their way into the wall. As they had grown over the revolutions, the masonry had eventually conceded its position and fallen outwards. It was these areas on which the alliance concentrated.

The Magta hacked at the tree trunks as the others started to haul the forgotten stones back into place. For the first time in most of their lives, the men folk stripped to the waist, as they toiled in the soaring temperatures.

Var found Hanelore near the apex of the pyramid. He had his divining pendulum and was consulting a tattered piece of parchment. He looked up into the sky and then drew lines across it with his fingers. He turned the piece of paper one hundred and eighty degrees, and scratched his head.

"Any ideas?" asked Var.

"It is only a guess young Var, but I believe that is still our star - Shu. If that is correct then as you can see it is much larger than before. I can therefore deduce that we are on another planet in our system. One that orbits much closer to our central star. It is just a hunch, but that seems to fit my findings. None of my instruments are working as they should, but I guess that is not surprising. It would make sense that if the creators thought moving to the moon would only provide a limited lifespan, then moving closer to the dying star would be a better option."

"But where are they?" asked Var.

"I think I may have the answer to that also" smiled the old giant. "Look through my spyglass." Hanelore placed the metal tube at Var's eye and turned his head to face in the direction of the Volcanoes. "Can you see it?"

"I can see the range of mountains. Is that what you mean?" replied Var.

"They are not mountains my boy. They are volcanoes. Gebshu had them once, but not as many as this. They may look like mountains, but they are far deadlier. They are connected to the heart of the planet. The fire which is the lifeblood of all living worlds flows within them. When the planet wakes and shakes its skin, these mountains will spew planet-fire into the skies."

Var looked at the giant and started to smile. The smile erupted into a laugh.

"That is not what I was pointing towards" said Hanelore, annoyed. "Can you see the volcano that has smoke coming from it? Well look to the right."

"Another fire breathing mountain" sniggered Var.

Hanelore snatched the looking glass back.

"That is not a volcano. That has a stepped appearance not unlike the one we are sitting upon. It is manmade. I would venture that is where we will find our answers."

"But to be able to see it from this distance it has to be the largest building ever constructed" said Var amazed.

"Yes it would" smiled the giant. "Now you and Gero are on water duty. They must have had access to it in order to build this place. We are going to need it if we intend to stay here. I wouldn't advise travelling outside of the city boundary. I have no idea what is making the sounds coming from the forest."

Outside the wall surrounding the central pyramid were stepped tiers. Most seemed to have contained homes or industrial complexes. The jungle had long since reclaimed these areas and only small patches of bare stone could be seen under the luscious green cloak. Var and Gero walked under a tall stone archway. The twisting vines around the supporting pillars were the only reason the crumbling masonry was still standing. The rest of the building that the convoluted entrance had once served now lay in piles of rubble. As they carefully climbed over the debris they saw a wide open space ahead.

It looked to have been a market or meeting place as it was a perfectly square area. It was surrounded by some three storey facades that were still standing. In the centre a selection of broken pillars surrounded a circular wall. The two men cast an excited glance at each other.

"A well" said Var.

"That's exactly what I was thinking" replied Gero.

As they neared the object their suspicions were upheld. The small wall surrounded a deep hole in the ground. Var grabbed a small stone and let it drop into the void. They listened carefully but the anticipated splash did not happen.

"We're not going to have the same old argument on this one are we?" said Gero as he started to un-loop the rope. Var peered into the hole.

"I guess not" he frowned.

With the rope firmly fixed around his waist Var climbed over the wall. Gero took the strain and Var slowly walked backwards down into the pit. The walls of the well were dry. Even as he moved away from the light there was no sign of any recent water on the walls. Var's artificial leg jarred as he tried to lower it and he realised he had reached the bottom. The stone on the floor was covered in a thin layer of mud. Water had flowed through here.

"I am at the bottom" shouted Var. His voice echoed off in several directions. "There is no water but it does look like there has been at some point. It maybe just rainwater or runoff."

The column of light from above illuminated the circle in

which he stood, but he could see no further. He struck the flint several times onto the dry cloth. The wrapped torch burst into flames and Var held it aloft. Tunnels ran in all directions out from the well base. Var crouched down and made his way into one of them. A short way in thin stone slabs were positioned in both sides of the tunnel. It looked as if they would hold a stone from above blocking the waterway. Mud and detritus had built up around the sluice gate.

Var was about to turn away when he noticed a white object amongst the debris. He bent over and grabbed the object. He pulled it and saw that it was connected. As he dragged the object free he quickly dropped it in disgust and stood quickly to move away thumping into the low ceiling. Var cursed under his breath, rubbing his head. The object was bone. A backbone. The wide splayed vertebrae had loosened the earth as he had pulled it free. It was the skull that now rocked upside down that had shocked the ocean man. Whatever it was, it was not human - similar in size but had what resembled a huge bird's beak with eye sockets on the side. Var hurried back to the light.

The warm air of the old square was a welcome change from the claustrophobic tunnels.

"Well?" said Gero

"Very funny" replied Var. The giant laughed at his own joke. "There is no standing water but there is a maze of waterways. It looks like water has flowed through recently, but it could just be rainwater. If this well was ever full then it was supplied from somewhere else. Oh and there is something else. I found the remains of something. I have no idea what it was, but it was not human or Magta, although it could have been similar in size."

"It was dead though?" asked Gero.

"Of course it was, just a skull" said Var.

"That's good. The last thing we need is some strange alien creature to worry about. Probably shouldn't mention this to the others. Our change in circumstances has been a major upheaval and it will take a while to adjust. One strange thing at a time."

"Yes. Agreed" replied Var. "We should probably try to find the start of the tunnels, they may lead us back to a water source." Var desperately wanted to change the topic. He couldn't get the ghostly skull from his mind.

The two friends made their way out from the square and down into the lower part of the city. They climbed through and over the remnants of the ancient city until they reached the outer wall. Even in its dilapidated state it was still impressive. Huge gaps were torn in the structure and the dense jungle had forced its way inside. The rounded tops of the walls were an indication that the wall had been much higher. Even at its current height it stood on a par with the great Fortress of Ages. Var walked to stand next to the colossal stonework.

"Keeping things in or keeping things out?" he posed.

"Let's keep moving" suggested Gero.

The giant grabbed one of the thick vines that criss-crossed the wall. He pulled it hard testing its strength. Satisfied he climbed upwards. Standing on top of the crumbling wall he had a clear view across the treetops. He surveyed the area before climbing back down.

"There is a valley to the North. If there is a river then that is our best bet" said Gero.

"That would mean going outside these walls" said Var stating the obvious.

"We can follow the wall along and then head down into the valley" replied Gero ignoring his friend. He pushed a branch to one side and climbed through the breach in the wall. Var drew one of his swords and pushed past the giant. The unique blade made easy work of the vegetation as Var hacked a path alongside the massive city wall. Var sliced through a large vine and as he grabbed it to push it aside he fell forwards into a trench.

"Are you alright?" called Gero.

Var had scuffed his knuckles but apart from that was unscathed. He had landed in a shallow stone clad ditch. The construction shot off in both directions, disappearing under the city wall and out into the jungle.

"I think this may have been the waterway" said Var excited. Gero climbed down into the shallow depression.

"I think you may be right. It seems to follow the contours of the land. This is a leat" said the giant.

Var started to cut his way along the disused waterway. It wound its way out into the jungle keeping a subtle incline. The two men increased their pace as they heard the definite sound of running water. They cleared their way and came out to a small river. A weir had been constructed across the river and a large holding pool spread out behind it. A single stone slab acting as a sluice gate had been lowered into place stopping the water from entering the city's irrigation system. Var had removed his jerkin and without a word of warning dived headlong into the cool water. He surfaced shaking his head.

"This is great! Are you not coming in?" asked Var.

"I think I'll give it a miss" said Gero. "I'm more interested in those." He gestured up into the river valley. On the far side, at the base of a fern clad rock face was a series of cave entrances. Var swam to the edge of the pool and then ran to catch up with the giant. As they approached Var pinched his nose.

"Ughh. What is that smell? Is that you?" squeaked Var. The giant turned. He was holding his nose also.

"It's coming from the caves. They must lead into the bowels of this planet. At least it smells that way" replied Gero. A thin yellow mist hovered in the mouths of the caves.

"What is it?" asked Var.

"Sulphur" replied Gero. "At least I think that is what Hanelore calls it. This planet has all those volcanoes. Perhaps these tunnels link into them. That would explain it."

Even from the distance at which they stood they could both clearly see that the entrances to the caves were free from foliage. The muddy entrances showed signs of habitation. Neither of them mentioned it and they both returned to the weir.

The metal workings that had once connected to the sluice gate had long since rusted away. Several small brown metal stubs were all that was left of the lifting mechanism. Gero jumped into the dry leat. He put his back against the stone slab and strained against it. It did not move. They examined the slab. It had a carved indent halfway down but apart from that it was smooth. The two men searched in the forest for suitable timber. Var quickly found a straight tree the thickness of his leg. A few well placed blows and the tree toppled into the undergrowth. As he chopped the unwanted branches from the trunk Gero appeared hauling a large tree. He man handled it into the lined waterway. He lifted a large stone from the bank and placed it in front of the slab. Var did likewise but angled his branch in from the top of the bank.

The whittled end fitted snugly into the recess. Positioning the lever against the stone sides Var pulled down on the end of the tree. He hung on the pole using all of his weight. The long lever slowly moved the stone slab from its resting place. As it moved water flooded under it and into the causeway. Gero thrust the larger tree into the gap and copied the action of his friend. As Gero forced the end of the tree trunk downward the sluice gate lifted clear and fell with a huge splash into the holding pool.

Before Gero could applaud his actions the rush of water had knocked him off his feet and was washing him at speed back towards the city. Laughing Var jumped into the torrent. The return journey took only moments as the water hurtled along the leat. A huge hand clamped against Var's outstretched limb and hauled him from the water.

"That was fun" said Var. He laughed as the giant rung the water from his beard.

They made their way back to the old square and knelt to peer into the well. The water could be heard running below.

"It will take a while to fill" suggested Var. "We should see if we can find any openings closer to the pyramid."

The two sodden friends made their way back towards the inner wall. As they approached the recently rebuilt gateway Bronsur came running out.

"Whatever it is you did, it worked!" she exclaimed. Jumping to hug Var. She pulled away as she felt his wet clothes and smiled at him. "Come, take a look at this." They followed her through the entrance and towards the base of the pyramid. The majority of the people had stopped working and were jumping and splashing in a large pool. Although only ankle deep, the water was gradually filling, what, judging by the broken statue at the centre, must have once been an ornate fountain.

"Well done. Without water, our time here could have become difficult" congratulated Hanelore. "As you can see we have almost finished patching the walls. The Emperor and his men have cleared the vegetation from the walkways. We now have a formidable defensive position should we need it."

Gero cast a concerned look at Var.

"What is it?" asked Hanelore. "What else did you find?"

"Nothing" said Var. "There was nothing else."

Chapter 8 - The Volith

Var sat with Gero halfway up the side of the stepped pyramid. The two had been deep in conversation until the smell of roasting meat had filtered its way up from the compound below. Earlier in the afternoon Lin had returned with her hunting party. They had shot four beasts. One was squat with short stubby legs and the others were taller four-legged animals that had twisted horns on top of their heads. The skinned animals were now slowly turning above several fire pits.

"I'm not sure what they will taste like" said Var.

"To be honest I do not care. I am starving. You'd better get there before me..." Gero's voice trailed off as he stood. He looked out beyond the city walls. Shu was beginning to set behind the mountains but a yellow fog that was rising through the jungle could still be seen clearly. It was thickest in the valleys but was slowly moving up towards them.

"More sulphur?" asked Var.

"It could be. If it is a sulphur mist then I hope it doesn't reach us here" replied Gero.

"Why not?"

"Because our stay here will be short-lived. We won't be able to breathe. We should warn the others get them up here. At least this could explain why there is no-one living here" said Gero.

"Does it? This city would have taken many seasons to build. Perhaps it only happens occasionally, else why would they have persisted with it. Maybe this fog does not reach as far as their new city..." Var turned to look out across the forest towards the city they had glimpsed earlier. It was Var's turn to cut short his sentence. Out in the distance towards the chain of volcanoes was an intense light. It looked as if a star had fallen from the heavens and landed atop the strange city. The radiant beacon flickered as if it were a fire being stoked.

"You know what this means" said Var.

"Yes" said Gero. "We have a long journey ahead of us. Come. We must warn the others. The cloud is fast approaching the outer walls. "

The two bounded down the many steps of the pyramid. As they reached the floor below it was apparent that the strange yellow fog had already been spotted by the guards on top of the defensive wall. Gero and Var ran to join the rest of the leaders above the main gateway.

"Any ideas?" asked Lothair.

"We think it is a sulphur cloud" replied Gero.

"How would you know that?" asked the Titan.

"You'll smell it soon enough" replied Gero. "Besides Var and I saw something similar this morning. It was creeping out from a few caves. We were much closer, there was no mistaking the smell."

"This planet has fire in its belly" started Hanelore. "What Gero has surmised would make sense. If it rises further we will have to evacuate the walls and move up onto the pyramid."

"That would leave us unprotected" demanded the Emperor.

"That it would. But nothing can survive in that mist" said Hanelore.

"Are you sure?" questioned the Emperor. "There seemed to be no end of wildlife in the jungle throughout the rotation. Where have they gone?"

"Also," pondered Var "What if the pyramid is not high enough. What then?"

"Then this will be a short lived exodus my friends" replied Hanelore.

"There is something else" said Var. "There is a bright light radiating from the other man made mountain we saw earlier. If there is a chance that the creators are still here, that seems like a fairly solid indication that someone is home."

"One thing at a time Var. We must make it through this night before we plan our next move" said the Emperor.

The assembled group watched as the creeping yellow fog spilled into the lower city. It poured like some luminescent liquid through the breaches in the outer wall. It washed around the buildings and trees but then seemed to stop as if it had finally filled to the required depth. They gazed at the cloud for some time as it ebbed in and out like an ethereal sea. Confident that it had reached its limit Var breathed out.

"Have you been holding your breath?" asked Gero.

"No" replied Var, his cheeks colouring. They all turned to return to the evening meal, all except the Emperor. He stood transfixed by the yellow cloud.

"What is it?" asked Var.

"I thought I saw something move within the fog" replied the Emperor. Var looked out across the ruins. He stood shoulder to shoulder with Vas for some time. Eventually he moved.

"I cannot see anything" said Var.

"I must have been hallucinating. I was obviously mistaken" said the Emperor.

A shrill screech rang out from the jungle, and a tree cracked as it fell somewhere out behind the yellow smokescreen.

"Maybe not" suggested Var.

*

The chilling howls continued through the night but apart from the disturbance it passed uneventful. As the morning light crested the mountains there was disagreement within the camp. Var and Gero were keen to get underway and start the journey to the city of light - as it had been christened. Whereas the ever thoughtful Hanelore and the practical Emperor were keen to prepare for the journey.

"We cannot make that distance in a rotation. If we are caught in the fog, all will be lost" stated the Emperor.

"I agree" said Var. "But, how are we going to know. What do we hope to achieve by staying here for longer. We have no way of avoiding the mist even if we wanted to. We don't even know how far it stretches. It may simply be localised" he argued.

"You are keen to be underway young Var, and that is understandable. The Emperor is right however, we must prepare for the journey. We are safe whilst we remain here. None of us want to encounter the creatures that we heard last night. If we make it to the city of light then this will be our home for the next five moons at least" explained Hanelore.

"Five!" exclaimed Var.

"I have an idea but we will need this time in order to prepare it. Patience my young friend. We have come a long way. The goal we seek is within our grasp. Do not be so eager to rush into the unknown" replied Hanelore.

Conceding the argument as he always knew he would, Var listened to the bizarre plan that the old giant had concocted. He had become used to Hanelore's schemes, and he had not once doubted the knowledge with which the old Titan had been bestowed, but this time he was unsure.

Once again the community was divided into working groups. Some were tasked to hunt once more, others to collect all unused clothing and the rest to find trees suitable for tapping. They had to collect sap as they had done back on Gebshu. Gero and Var opted for the latter.

The trees that formed the dense jungle were diverse, all of them dwarfing the small pines back on the ocean planet. In the valleys there were wide leaved trees with gnarled trunks and massive canopies, whilst on the ridges were tall straight trees with needles instead of leaves. It was these that the working group concentrated on.

Var and Gero walked through the forest. The floor was covered in dead pine needles. The smell was pleasant and the decaying carpet gave a springy step as they made their way past countless suitable trees. Gero had seen the same thing as his friend and they were heading towards it. One of the trees had fallen. It had smashed an opening by knocking others over on its journey to the ground. What was unusual was that it had snapped a third of the way up and the fresh white timber inside stood out from a distance.

They arrived at the foot of the broken tree. The fallen section was still attached at the break by a few wooden fibres and created a triangle with the ground. Gero nudged it with his shoulder. The tree creaked and the giant jumped backwards.

"I don't think it will hold. We'll have to climb the trunk" said Gero.

Neither of them had any idea what they were looking for. Trees fall all the time. But they both knew this was unusual. Var nominated himself for the climb and threw a rope around the tree. He wrapped each end around his wrists and leant back. Keeping an acute angle he flipped the rope up and dug his feet in against the tree. He continued the process and slowly made his way up the trunk. As he neared the break he reached for the splintered edge. Straining he pulled himself up so that he was lying on his stomach across the severed tree.

"What can you see?" called Gero. Var looked down at his friend.

"You'll have to see this. Stand clear" he yelled. Taking his sword in one hand Var hacked at the bent timber that still connected to the fallen part of the tree. The blade sliced through the compressed timber and with a deafening crack it crashed to the floor. Var carefully moved back off the trunk and used the rope lasso to slide back to the floor. Gero was already examining the tree.

Four huge claw marks had ripped through the bark just above the break. Gero was placing his hand in one of them.

"There is another further up" indicated Var. The two examined the tree in silence and then searched the area for more signs of whatever had caused the damage. The ground was disturbed in many places but there was no clear evidence.

"Whatever did this has some strength" said Gero. "To snap a tree as if it were a twig."

"Do you think this is what we heard last night? That whatever it is can live in the sulphurous fog?" asked Var.

"I have no intention of finding out" stated Gero. "We'd best get on with collecting sap, or whatever is out here will be the least of our worries."

"True" said Var. "Your father can be scary at times."

Var and Gero returned late in the afternoon with a full pot of the sticky pungent liquid. They were happy to see more of the long legged creatures over the fire. The smaller stocky animal had been incredibly tough and stringed with gristle. Laid out across the lower steps of the pyramid was a huge piece of cloth. The patchwork ensemble had been carefully created by stitching garment after garment together. Further along some of the Dumonii were putting the finishing touches to a giant circular basket. It had been woven together using thin pliable branches and was perfectly round with a hole at the centre.

"We made good progress, maybe three more moons and we will be ready" said Hanelore as he inspected the craftsmanship of the Dumonii.

Var ignored the giant as he started to demonstrate his concept to the others. He wound his way through the busy neighbourhood to find Bronsur helping carve the evening meal. She smiled as he approached.

"This meat is good. Makes a healthy change from all that fish" said Bronsur.

"I like fish" complained Var. The couple sat and ate together. All the while Var was debating internally whether to confide in Bronsur. He decided not to. "I think we should bed down up in the gateway tonight. Hopefully it will be a bit quieter inside. I really need to get a good night's sleep" moaned Var.

"Of course" soothed Bronsur.

Var sat on the edge stone by the doorway to the shimmer gateway, whilst Bronsur made a suitable place to sleep just inside. Var watched as the light faded and the yellow mist crept towards them through the trees once more. The screeches followed shortly behind. This time they seemed more frequent, louder and maybe it was his imagination but they seemed fevered. His eyelids felt heavy and he allowed his head to fall into his hands.

Shouts and screams woke the sleeping Doyen. Even in the darkness he could see the problem. The yellow mist had enveloped the lower city and was lapping against the inner wall below. He bolted upright.

"Stay here Bron. I'll go and see what's happening."

Var leapt from step to step as he hurried to the base of the pyramid. As he neared the bottom he gasped as he saw one of the guards on the walls disappear over the edge. His scream echoed around the city ruins. Var ran to the wall and climbed the steps three at time. Drawing both his swords he hurried towards Gero.

"What's happening?" asked Var.

"There are creatures in the fog. Don't get too close to the edge" he warned. Var leaned forward slightly trying to get a glimpse of the mysterious animals. As he did a hideous visage leapt up from the swirling fog. Its long claws clutching onto the battlements. Gero's axe thumped into the stone severing the creature's hand. The giant's boot followed, crashing into the creature's face and sending it flying back into the mist. The dissected hand twitched and wiggled as dark blood oozed from the wound. Var kicked the amputated hand out into the darkness.

"What in the name of the Gods was that!" exclaimed Var.

"Just another creature that wants to kill us it seems. Do you ever get the feeling that perhaps the Gods do not want to talk with us?" replied Gero. He wiped the blood from his axe blade and sniffed his fingers. "Yuk. They smell as bad on the inside, but at least we know we can kill them."

The creatures of the mist were known as the Volith. They were indigenous to the planet. They had adapted to the volcanic structure of the world. Their unique metabolism allowed them to breathe the toxic sulphuric fumes, whilst in contrast the warm night air was harmful to them. As the deep underground chambers vomited the yellow gas into the night the Volith rampaged within it hunting as far as the fog would take them.

They stood just shorter than the Magta. They resembled early primates with huge muscled shoulders and arms. They could run on all four limbs using their knuckles or walk upright, but they preferred to transfer from branch to branch within the forest. At the top of the thickset neck was a domed head. The creature had a curved bone central beak that ran from the back of its head and then protruded down over its lower lip. It's mouth was packed full of haphazard serrated teeth. It had yellow eyes on either side of its head, with a vertical black line as an iris. Two small breathing holes on top of its beak completed the strange beast.

Over its shoulders and across its chest it had large scales. The hard lizard like skin continued all over its body with the scales reducing in size towards its extremities. Pearlescent green and yellow hues decorated its armature. The primitive creature lacked any real intelligence, but nature had compensated for this deficiency by giving the Volith a considerable arsenal and making it the apex predator. They moved with incredible speed following the ebb and flow of the yellow mist. Luckily for the defenders the sulphuric fog had settled its level just below the wall.

Another animal leapt onto the battlements in front of Var as the yellow cloud billowed upwards. It watched the ocean warrior closely with its reptile eyes. A scaled eyelid closed and opened slowly cleaning the iris. It threw its head back and screeched. Var shuddered as he saw the rows of teeth and the flicking forked tongue. The sound seemed to ripple back through the fog as if they were communicating with each other.

It lashed out and Var swept his kopesh downwards. The incisive blade cut deeply into the animal's huge forearm. Undeterred by the wound it pressed onward lowering its head and ramming Var in the chest. Var dropped one of his swords into the compound as he sprawled backwards across the battlements. The creature leapt towards him. Instinctively Var brought his legs up to protect himself. At the same time he lunged out with his sword. The heavy creature fell on him. Its own weight causing Var's blade to penetrate deep into its body. Mortally wounded the creature howled as it still tried to tear at its prey. Var shifted his weight and pushing up with his legs succeeded in throwing the Volith down into the compound. As it thumped into the ground several waiting soldiers sank their swords into its already dead body.

Var shouted to the Dumonii warrior below, who obliged in throwing Var's sword back up to him. He looked across for Gero. The burly giant was sweating in the warm night air. Green blood dripped from both edges of his axe.

All along the wall the defenders battled furiously whenever the fog fluctuated and crested the battlements.

Suddenly the screeching ceased. It was replaced by a clacking sound like the creatures were thumping their feet or slapping their skin. The reason for the change soon became apparent. Out into the distance several huge shapes could be seen wading through the mist. One stopped and raised itself up on its back legs. It was identical to the smaller Volith except it was three times the size. It threw its arms back and roared. The bass call reverberated through the ground. Ducking its head back into the fog it continued towards them.

"I think we've found what toppled that tree" said Gero.

The huge creature reared up in front of them, its head level with the top of the wall. It lashed out, slamming its fist into the battlements. Shockwaves sent Var toppling as he looked to avoid the other arm. The giant Volith ripped the battlements away as it sought to climb onto the wall.

Gero rolled forward and as he came to his feet he swung his axe. The butterfly blades bit deeply into the creature's shin. The Volith punched downwards. Gero avoided the blow but had to leave his weapon embedded in the creature's leg. Var leapt in to distract the giant animal. The creature swung its hand trying to swat the small prey in front of it. Var stepped back and slashed at the swinging fist. His blades drew red tracks across the creature's knuckles.

The animal looked down at Gero who was trying to regain his axe. It reached down quickly and grabbed the Magta warrior. Gero yelled as the creature tried to crush him. His old wounds flared with pain. Lothair had seen the huge creature crest the wall and was running to assist. His hammer glowed as he leapt in the air. In a blue blur the hammer cracked into the kneecap of the Volith. The beast felt the blow and staggered. Before it could respond, Lothair thundered another blow in at exactly the same point. This time the hammer head shattered bone. The Volith screeched in pain, dropping Gero. As he landed he tore his axe free and moved through the legs of the great animal. He brought the axe up behind his head and sliced downwards. The savage blow ripped through the Volith's Achilles tendon and the creature fell backwards. As it toppled from the battlements its massive clawed hand reached out and took Lothair with it into the yellow sea.

Further along the wall the second of the giant beasts had attacked. It too had climbed onto the wall. The Emperor and his Dominators had tried to fight it back, but it charged forward. The Dominators scattered and the Volith tumbled down into the compound. Archers up on the Pyramid launched a volley of arrows at the furious animal. Most clattered harmlessly from its tough scaly hide, The occasional shaft found a softer target and buried home. Undeterred by the annoying stings the Volith simply rubbed its skin breaking the arrows off. The creature shifted its head from side to side looking for its next victim. It stopped briefly and seemed to cough. Out from the sulphuric air even this formidable animal started to suffer. It coughed again and looked to get back to safety of the yellow cloud. The Emperor noticed the change in the animal.

"It is struggling to breathe away from the mist. Keep it here and we can kill it" he yelled. Oma-Sem grabbed a spear and ran to the edge of the wall. He leapt into the air using his body weight as well as his arm to launch the weapon. His aim was true and the shaft punctured the softer scales around its stomach. Oma-Sem landed heavily twisting his ankle. As he tried to rise the creature ran towards him and batted him across the courtyard. The creature turned its back on the wall eyeing its downed prey. The Emperor ran and jumped. Bringing his wide blade up in both hands he landed on the back of the Volith ramming the sword in between its shoulder blades. The creature roared flinging its arms back. Vas held on and shifting his weight upwards drove the weapon deeper. The remaining Dominators leapt into the compound and hacked at the creatures legs. It buckled and then toppled to the ground succumbing to the clean air and its injuries. The Emperor rode the animal as it fell and rolled on his shoulder as it neared the ground. He grabbed the hilt of his sword and pulled it free. Green blood spurted from the wound. Lifting the blade aloft he chopped down across the dying creature's neck. In a flurry of strikes the head eventually lolled and parted company with its body. A cheer rang out amongst the Dominators.

A third giant Volith had caused significant damage further along the wall. The Dumonii and Ocean tribes had struggled to contain it or even injure it. They had fallen back to the pyramid after their losses had continued to rise. They had been surprised that the animal did not pursue them and were grateful for the respite. This knowledge spread quickly through the defenders and they gradually withdrew to the safety of the ziggurat. Var and Gero were the last two on the wall.

They had fought off wave after wave of creatures that had managed to scale the wall, desperately trying to get a glimpse of Lothair. Gero swung his axe upwards thunking the blade into a creatures midriff. Letting go with one hand he swung his fist, cracking it into the beaked face of the loathsome creature. As it sailed over the edge he put his foot on the edge of the battlements and called out for his brother. There was no reply.

Var put a hand on the giant's arm.

"Gero, we must withdraw, he is lost."

Gero was about to turn when he saw a flash of blue light within the mist.

"He lives!" bellowed the giant.

Var went to the inside edge and beckoned for a rope. The thick cordage was thrown up over the wall.

"Hold this tight!" shouted Var.

Gero had already thrown the other end down into the mist.

"Lothair! This way my brother. Climb the rope" called Gero.

The rope went taught and Gero flexed ready. Lothair's helmeted head poked through the mist. He climbed quickly and Gero reached down to grab his outstretched arm. The Titan was covered in green blood and Gero struggled to keep his grip on the slippery armour. Lothair smiled as he cleared the fog but then a clawed hand leapt upwards grabbing hold of his ankle. The sudden shock of weight nearly took both giants into the yellow mire, but Gero dug his heels in against the stonework and pulled back.

"Pull!" he yelled to the men holding the rope below him. The concerted effort hauled Lothair and the attached Volith upwards. As they neared the edge Var slashed his blade across the creature's arm rending it in two. Those pulling fell backwards. Gero, Lothair and Var dropped down into the compound and ran to join the others on the pyramid steps.

"That was close" said Lothair. "Thank you for waiting brother."

"You always were a bit slow when it came to combat, so I thought I would give you a while longer" replied Gero. Lothair slapped him on the shoulder.

"Thank you too, young Var" said Lothair.

Var was staring down. Lothair followed his gaze and noticed the cleaved Volith's hand was still firmly clamped around his ankle. He reached down and pried the fingers apart and the dead appendage bounced down the pyramid.

"These are going to be a long couple of moons" said Var.

No-one slept that night. The remaining people moved all belongings up into the gate chamber. whilst the warriors sat and watched the baying creatures as they continued to tear at the wall. Several more of the giant Volith had appeared and had made significant holes in the defensive structure. Realising that their prey had moved to safety, the edge of the yellow mist quietened and the Volith slunk back into the night.

*

As the welcome warm light of morning embraced the tired people they prepared to clean up the aftermath. To their horror the killing ground in front of the wall was devoid of anything. There were no bodies to be seen of either side. There were dried red and green blood stains covering the stone floor and walls but that was the only sign of battle remaining.

Work on Hanelore's scheme continued in earnest. No-one wanted to spend another night in the fated city. Everything was moved up onto the pyramid. The people of the alliance moved into the darkness of the shimmer gateway. The plan was to simply avoid the Volith. They prayed that the mist could not rise higher than it had. If it did, then they would defend the four narrow entrances.

The wounded were treated and those with serious injuries were allowed to rest. Those who could joined in the effort to complete the tasks. Inevitably Shu set once more behind the jagged mountain chain and the warriors of the stranded people of Gebshu prepared for another night of torment. They watched as the yellow fog rose from the wooded valleys. To their immense relief it settled lower down in the city. The screeching from the creatures of the mist now washed over them as they tried to sleep.

The following night also gave them respite as the fog only reached the heads of valleys. Hanelore had guessed it was like a natural tide. The depths of the planet spewed a certain volume of sulphuric vapour each night and when exhausted it would settle. The old Titan had spent the last two moons searching the ruins of the city in the hope the ancient Dumonii settlers had charted the depth of the fog. He found nothing.

As the light faded on the third rotation the people moved the completed equipment up into the pyramid for safety. The round baskets were too large to fit inside so were roped at the top of the pyramid.

Var helped finish lashing the baskets and sat looking out towards the city of light. Gero dumped himself next to his friend.

"One more night. That's all my friend. Then we will make our way towards the city" said Gero.

"Let us pray it is a quiet night. The people have been through so much. I had no idea what to expect when we reached the Pillars. Now here we are on another planet. We have escaped the icy death of Gebshu only to replace it with something far worse. It seems as if there is no end" said Var.

"There is an end to everything, at least one way or another. I have to say I do not miss my old life. From the day I met you on Vormerian's Spine it has been one non-stop adventure."

"I'm sorry Gero. I did not meant to drag you into all this" replied Var.

"Dragged me. I hardly think so. The last seasons of

my life have been the best of my life. I had wallowed in self pity for long enough. Now when I eventually make my way to the depths I will do so knowing I have lived my life. I have fought for what was right, and my heart beats with contented pride. If anything little Var you have set me free."

"What about your father and your brother? Do you think they regret coming with us?" asked Var.

"My brother, like you, worries for his people. If they had remained they would be slaves to the Mer or worse. At least here the last of the Magta can shout defiance at the universe. He knows our time is over, you and the Dumonii are the future. He will ensure legends reflect the Magta in a heroic light. As for my father. There is a fine line between genius and madness. I feel he can switch between the two at will. That makes it somewhat difficult to read him. I know this though, in his mind he is still young. He craves the past but lives in the present knowing his body cannot keep pace with his wits."

"We are all children on the inside" said Var. "We all hide it deep within us, but I don't mind admitting there is a frightened child in my heart."

"Well then, its well past his bedtime. Come let's get back to the others. You are starting to depress me" chuckled Gero.

The dreaded yellow mist rose swiftly that evening crashing over the outer walls and filling the lower city even before the light of Shu had faded. The mist kept drifting upwards and to the onlookers' alarm its wispy fingers flowed over the inner wall and into their compound. Dark shapes followed in its wake. The poisoned fog lapped the pyramid steps and started to climb.

Several archers loosed arrows blindly into the vapour.

"Hold your fire!" roared the Emperor. "Save your arrows. Only fire when you have a clear target. Aim for the throat and belly; anything else will be a waste."

With all civilians inside the gateway, the combined warriors filled each doorway. They would fight three abreast with plenty of others behind them ready to take their places if they fell. Most of the Magta Destructors, Gero, Lothair and Var stood on the step just above the entrances. They had to protect the baskets. In behind stood the Emperor and his Dominators. They were ready to plug any holes in the Magta lines. Positioned in and around the baskets were Lin and a hand-picked team of archers.

As the fog continued to rise Var dropped to his knees. He placed his swords on the stone and bowed his head forward.

"Please hear my prayer. In the hardships we have faced I have not once asked for your help. I ask for it now. Grant us the courage to see this night through. Give us the strength to stand tall and welcome the morning light once more."

"To whom are you praying?" asked Gero.

"Anyone who'll listen" replied Var.

"The Gods have forsaken us Var, I fear your words fall on deaf ears. Sharp steel and the loyal company of your brothers in arms will see us through. Let us rip the hearts from these beasts and make them rue the day they sought our wrath" said the Emperor.

"Well at least someone was listening" whispered Gero.

The fighting erupted on all four sides of the pyramid. The mist had settled only a couple of steps below the entrances. It was close enough for the Volith to brave excursions into the fresh air.

The defenders had the advantage of height. It was easier to swing downwards as the creatures tried to climb. Swords and pole-arms sliced and pummelled the advancing Volith and the line held firm. The skirmishes continued until well past midnight. There was no concerted attack, they seemed to attack randomly, screeching at each other before darting towards the wall of blades. The alliance had lost only a few men whilst they had inflicted heavy losses. With a lull in the fighting Lothair removed his helm and wiped the sweat from his brow. Despite the darkness it was still warm.

Then the thing they had feared the most came roaring up the pyramid. The giant Volith reached the edge of the mist and screamed a challenge against the miniscule prey that stood against it. Two others appeared on the other slopes and joined the sickening chorus.

"This is it!" yelled Lothair. "Kill these and the night is ours."

As the massive creature pounded its forearms on the steps to climb out from the fog, Lothair jumped high into the air. With his soul-drinking hammer raised high he forged it downwards. The powerful blow fragmented the beast's skull. Bone shards dug deep into its brain and it flopped forwards as its final breath escaped. As Lothair landed a swarm of Volith rose from the mist. He made to swing his hammer but he could not lift it fast enough. One creature charged the Titan knocking him from his feet. It pinned his arm and sunk its teeth into his shoulder. It bit through his metal armour as if it were linen. Arrows peppered the creature. It released its bite and looked upwards. A long black arrow shaft punched into its chest killing it instantly. Hanelore had joined Lin and her archers. Not even the tough scales of a Volith could withstand the power of the Nightsigh. Gero dragged his brother back inside the pyramid, before returning to the fight.

The two other giant Volith were making serious dents in the defenders' numbers. One had started to pound the doorway to the South. Masonry exploded in all directions as the door collapsed crushing the Dumonii warriors beneath it. A Magta warrior dove from the higher steps, a short sword in each outstretched hand. He choked as the

Volith reached up and caught him in mid-air. The courageous warrior stabbed the creature once in the back of the hand before its gaping maw closed over his head. With one twist the creature ripped his head from his body. It threw the decapitated body back into the mists.

The huge monster continued to batter the warriors despite the many arrows and broken shaft sticking out from its body. Var ran along the narrow ledge towards the giant animal. He shouted to the Emperor.

"Keep it busy."

Vas nodded and picking up a discarded shield he hurled it at the Volith. The missile cannoned off its beak cracking a few teeth. The Emperor dived to the side as a fist clubbed into the masonry where he had just been. The Emperor now had the animal's undivided attention. It brought its arms down in a blur, like it was hammering out a frenzied drum beat. The last thump caught the Emperor on the shoulder plates knocking him to the floor. He raised his sword waiting for the death blow.

After a moment of inaction he looked up to see Var had jumped into the beast. A blade in each hand he hung onto each one as his bodyweight pulled them downwards through the animals stomach. The two incisions tore open the Volith's abdomen and its intestines spilled out on top of Var. The Dominators swarmed over the injured animal and within moments it twitched as the final blow separated its vertebrae.

The final mammoth creature was also beginning to falter. Green blood oozed from hundreds of cuts and gashes. Sore patches covered its shoulders where its protected scales had been torn and cut away. It had gripped a Magta warrior by the ankle and was dragging him into the mist. Hanelore fired another black arrow from the Nightsigh punching into its arm. The Volith looked up at its tormentor and howled. As it screeched its hatred the old Titan loosed another shaft. The arrow entered the Volith's open mouth and burst out through the back of its head. The beast fell into the stone. Its large reptile eye fixating on Hanelore. With one last act of defiance it managed to throw the trapped Magta warrior it still had in its grasp back out into the unseen ravenous pack. Its eyelid closed just before another black arrow punctured its eye socket.

With the alpha males defeated the screeching horde of Volith lost their courage and their appetite. They slowly slunk back into the bubbling mists.

"Looks like your prayers have been answered" said Gero.

"If we make it through tomorrow night, then I will know for sure that the Gods are with us" smiled Var.

Chapter 9 - Flight

As the mist slowly receded the last people of Gebshu set about their tasks. They would need every possible moment of light. As before there was no sign of bodies on the steps of the pyramid, just the gruesome blood trails, where the dead and dying had been dragged back into the jungle. A sombre mood hung over the camp and no-one voiced the fear they were all feeling. Var found Hanelore staring through his scope out towards their destination.

"You should get that thing permanently attached to your face" suggested Var.

"Quite" said Hanelore. "It doesn't matter how long I stare, I cannot gauge our route any better than I have. The majority of the city of light is obscured by the wooded hills in between. I cannot tell if the forest stretches to its gates or ends over the far hill. I guess it matters not, as we have no idea how far the mist travels."

"Can we make it before it gets dark?" asked Var.

"No we cannot. Even at the fastest pace I estimate we could make it perhaps a fifth of the way before nightfall. Our only hope lies with these crude contraptions." Hanelore gestured towards the circular baskets that were being rolled from the pyramid.

"You have planned as best you could. We are grateful that we have any hope of escaping this place. I personally would rather take my chances with anything else than remain here another night. You never know the fog may only reach a few hills away and we will be clear of danger by mid afternoon" suggested Var.

"The optimism of youth" laughed the old giant.

As they climbed down the crumbling stone steps, Var looked at the gathering people below. They had left Asturia with just over one thousand people. There were barely four hundred remaining. The night's fighting had seriously depleted the number of warriors. Civilians now outnumbered those who could bear arms. Even though most of those remaining, including the women and the children had armed themselves and were prepared to fight, another battle would be their last.

Once again the alliance had separated out into groups. One group consisting of mainly warriors had already left. They were hacking a trail into the jungle. Another was rolling the huge baskets and another carrying the long folded material. The injured would file in behind, with a smaller group of warriors taking up the rear, which included Var and Gero.

As they crossed through a broken section of the outer wall, Var looked back at the doomed ruin.

"You can't be sorry to leave this place?" said Gero.

"No definitely not. I am hoping we don't ever see it again" said Var.

"Yes I agree. That is another reason I am glad you are not leading this column" said Gero.

"What do you mean?" asked Var hurt by the giant's comment.

"Well, what with your half leg. You would probably lead us around in a circle. I can see it now. Oh look. A forgotten city. It looks very similar to the one we had been trapped in for the last four moons."

Var laughed.

"That may be true. But do you know why Hanelore asked you to be at the back with me?" replied Var.

"For protection, obviously" said Gero.

"That's not what your father told me" said Var tramping down a fern. Gero didn't reply. Var waited. He knew the giant couldn't leave it alone.

"Go on then" said Gero. "What did he say?"

"He said that the reason you could not lead the group was that you would stop at every bush that bore fruit to have a bite to eat." Var skipped forward avoiding Gero's swipe. "Oh look" shouted Var pointing at a brightly coloured blossom. "That looks tasty."

The column made good progress throughout the morning. The warriors on point were making short work of clearing the way. Apart from the few hills they had to climb the following procession had kept up the demanding pace. As the front party crested yet another hill Hanelore asked Lin to scout the next leg. Lin leapt into a nearby tree and within moments had scaled it. She returned back to the ground as the first of the wheels appeared, coming up the hill.

"What can you see?" asked Hanelore.

"More of the same" replied Lin. "It seems endless. There is another hill like the one we are on before another that is much higher. It blocks the view beyond."

"Can we make it before dusk?" asked Hanelore.

"I guess we'll have to" replied Lin.

"This is it then. We have to speed up our progress. We must get there well before the others arrive if we are to prepare. Pass the message along the line that Var and my son and their rearguard are needed at the front. The more of us there are the better chance we stand" said Hanelore.

The request filtered back through the column and Var, Gero and the others increased their pace and started to overtake the other groups. As they made it to the front they broke into a slow jog. They soon caught up with Hanelore and the Emperor. They climbed the second steeper hill and Lin once again obliged by climbing the tallest tree. The message was the same. Hiding his disappointment Hanelore barked out instructions.

The warriors now used their weapons against the forest. They hacked at the trees clearing a large area on top of the spur. Hanelore directed the harvesting. Any trees that the old giant had marked were cut some distance up the trunk rather than at the base like the others. These marked trunks formed crude circles. All of the felled timber was stacked in the centre of these four wooden henges.

The light had started to fade and although verging on exhaustion, they continued to work as fast they could. They all knew what was at stake. As the baskets arrived they were lifted and placed on top of the specially cut trees. The huge fabric sheets were hauled into place across the holes in the wooden baskets. They had been constructed as massive envelopes and the open ends were lashed to the woven base whilst the majority of the material hung over the edge.

As soon as the first one had been securely tied in place, Hanelore ordered the felled timber at the centre to be lit. The freshly cut leaves and needles crackled and popped as the heat increased. Smoke billowed upwards. As previously decided the alliance contingent had split into four groups. Each stood by their respective fire. They had also split the leadership. The Emperor had insisted that be the case. Practical to the last.

Gero and Var led one, Hanelore, Lothair and the Emperor the others. It was Lothair's construction that was ready first. The assembled group had climbed into the basket and were busy organising themselves so that they counterbalanced each other. The wood in the central fire was now in full flame. The hot air had now inflated the patchwork balloon and it wavered above their heads. The basket started to creak as the canopy tried to lift it clear. Four tethers held it in place as the superheated air rose to fill the balloon completely. Satisfied that the colossal stitched bag could hold no more the strained ropes were cut. The balloon soared swiftly into the air. The assembled riders pulled on the ropes around the open mouth, sealing the envelope.

A massive cheer rang out across the hillside as the first of the air balloons drifted high up into the sky.

"Now we have to pray the wind will guide us" said Hanelore as he watched the circular blob move away. "It is travelling North. That is good. Quickly get the fire going" ordered the old Titan.

Shu had set. The yellow mist and the hellish screams that accompanied it started to wash through the valleys. It filled each in turn before slowly rising upwards. The previous hill that they had crossed was being submerged just as Var and Gero's balloon took to the sky. It was followed shortly after by the Emperor. As they ascended they watched in trepidation as Hanelore's envelope had still not filled to capacity. From their vantage point they could see the yellow sea slowly rising. The highest peaks were now islands in the poisonous fog. They could see dark shapes moving within it.

The mist crept up towards the last balloon. Hanelore looked up at the twisting envelope. He looked at the creatures only a short distance away. He cursed.

"Cut the ropes!" he yelled.

As the tethers were cut the balloon rose quickly. Yellow mist swirled around beneath them as the Volith climbed the cut trees and tried to jump to the basket. Luckily they were too high for the smaller creatures but a giant Volith came running on all fours towards them. Using the tree trunks as a springboard it leapt into the air. Its outstretched hand grabbed onto the basket. Its weight flung the basket to one side and those not firmly secured fell into the churning eddies below. The creature's huge mass was slowly pulling the balloon back down.

Hanelore notched an arrow to the Nightsigh and ran to where those still on board were trying to hack at the fingers of the creature. He pulled back the bow string and loosed the arrow. It punched into its chest piercing one of its hearts. The Volith's fingers lifted and the howling beast fell back into the yellow clouds below. The release of weight sent the balloon soaring upwards and lurched again. Hanelore was thrown from the basket. He managed to grab one of the dangling ropes as he fell. The jolt tore at his shoulder and the priceless bow spiralled out from his grip.

He gripped the swaying rope with his other arm as the pain flared in his ruined shoulder. Those on the basket above tried to pull the old Titan to safety. They struggled as the wind buffeted them from side to side.

Hanelore looked up into the concerned faces above.

"Tell my sons to remember me in their songs." With that the old giant released his grip and fell.

*

Unaware of the tragedy that had unfolded on the last balloon Var and Gero slapped each other on the backs as they watched the fourth canopy follow them up into the sky. It cruised at a much lower height than the other three. Despite losing a third of its passengers the envelope was only partly full.

They looked towards the bright beacon of the city of light. Relieved the wind was carrying them in the right direction they tried to scan the distance. They could not make out any detail in the low light but the dark shapes of the forest seemed to end some way ahead. The city sat away from the chain of volcanoes in the middle of what appeared to be a plain or a desert. Spirits on board three of the air craft lifted.

"You know what you said about Hanelore" started Var. "Well I can say it is definitely madness. Only a madman could dream up something like this. Where do his ideas come from?"

"I have no idea. He told me once that we all remain

scholars until our final day. Anyone who thought that they had nothing left to learn was a fool. He always has his head buried in some historic tome or other such ancient text. We'll have to ask him when we land" replied Gero.

"That's another thing. How do we land?" said Var.

"There are two ways apparently. We can open the mouth of the canopy and release the air. Or eventually the air inside will cool and then we will come down" said Gero raising his eyebrows.

"Only one of those we have control over" indicated Var. Gero looked at his friend with renewed nervousness. Bronsur clambered towards them.

"Careful Bron, make sure you hold on. The wind could topple us if you are not careful" warned Var.

"Stop your worrying. You are worse than my mother" scorned Bronsur.

"I wonder what's happening to them?" said Var.

"They will be safe in Asturia. With the Mer gone they can resume a normal life, as least for the time being" replied Bronsur.

"Heh. A normal life. Remember that?" laughed Gero.

"Not for some time" laughed Var. Bronsur snuggled into his arms and the three looked to the future as they peacefully flew above the sprawling jungle.

The prevailing winds carried the four balloons towards their fate as the night passed. The white glow behind the mountains indicated that dawn was fast approaching. Lothair's balloon was furthest ahead and they could now see an end to the forest. Ahead the trees thinned and the land rose into a barren plateau. What appeared to be sand dunes waded into the jungle-scape and the sulphurous mist thinned as it met them.

Judging by their height Lothair was confident that they would clear the edge of the jungle. He looked back at the others. He swallowed as he saw the last balloon was already dangerously low and the other two were falling quickly.

The Titan didn't get a chance to see the fate of the others as they suddenly plummeted. Clinging on to the basket they watched as the tree canopies shot past beneath them. As they neared the edge of the forest the balloon lurched upwards. Several passengers fell as the basket swung almost vertical. As they crested the first dunes the envelope started to collapse on itself and they crashed into the sand.

Checking that most of his crew were uninjured by the harsh landing, Lothair ran back towards the jungle.

Var and Gero looked on helplessly as Hanelore's basket clipped a particularly tall tree sending it into a spin. Within moments the fabric envelope tore as it clattered into the forest. The basket and all its passengers disappeared into the mist.

"He'll be okay" said Var. "It will be light soon. The mist is already retreating. We can get to him in time."

The two remaining balloons were now caught in the downdraft that had grabbed hold of Lothair's. Var wound the rope around his wrist as their speed increased. They hurtled towards the treetops and the basket jumped and bucked in the turbulence. They saw the sand in between the trees and realised they were almost safe. As they neared the large sand slope to the plateau, the winds grabbed at them, once more ripping the balloon upwards. The strain on the ropes that held it to the basket were already fatigued and several snapped. The basket swung down spilling its live cargo. Bronsur flew past Var screaming. Var reached out and grabbed her but he only succeeding in clutching her sleeve. It tore free and she fell.

"Bron!" cried Var as he watched her flail at the air. They were still a way above the trees but if they landed in the sand there was a slim chance they could survive the fall. Var didn't get the chance to see as the basket slammed into the top of the dunes smashing it to pieces. He was thrown clear and thumped heavily into the sand. Gero had been unable to release his grip and was being dragged along with the remnants of the envelope. The wind had caught it and was playing with its new toy. Pain flared in the giant's wrist as the rope rubbed away his skin. He reached for his boot knife and sawed at the restraint.

The remaining woven sticks of the basket and the tattered patchwork canopy quickly vanished out across the desert. He spat sand from his mouth and shook it from his beard. There were people and debris spread out in a long line from where the balloon had impacted at the edge of the dunes. He made his way back checking on those he passed. When he reached the top of the steep sandy incline he saw that the Emperor had not been so lucky.

The top of the makeshift envelope could be seen a short way out into the jungle. He looked down the slope and saw Var running between the bodies. Encouragingly some of them were moving. Some had survived the fall. He ran to join his friend passing the white dead trunks of trees that were being slowly digested by the ever moving sand dunes.

"She's not here!" cried Var in panic. They made their way further into the periphery of the jungle checking each body as they moved. Then Var froze. To his right, up above in one of the dead tree trunks lay a body draped over one of its branches. He knew instantly it was Bronsur. He dropped to his knees in utter defeat and sadness. Gero stood by him. He looked out into the jungle. The yellow mist was slowly creeping backwards.

"I am truly sorry my friend, but I must go and search for my father" said the giant. He waited a moment for a reply he knew would not be forthcoming, before loping off into the jungle.

The Emperor opened his eyes. He had been knocked out as they had crashed into the tree tops. He felt pain in his ankle and his head throbbed. He looked up to see that his foot had been caught in the tree branches and that he was dangling upside down. He heard screeches and shouts from below and he could make out the survivors from the crash running in all directions as the Volith stalked them. He grimaced as he watched one of his Dominators round a tree, straight into a waiting beast. The creature bit down on his neck and blood sprayed over the animal's beak.

Vas strained his stomach muscles pulling his upper body high enough for him to grab the branch above. He twisted his foot and pulled it free. He climbed quickly down the tree ignoring the pain from his ankle. As he neared the ground he reached under his breastplate and tore his undershirt away. He wrapped it around his nose and mouth and dropped to the ground. The Volith was gorging itself on the dead Dominator and did not notice as the Emperor's blade clove into its back. As it spun from the blow the Emperor kicked it in the chest. It thudded into a stump. He ran at the animal and thrust his sword into its stomach. The blow pinned the flailing animal to the broken tree.

As the Emperor tried to pull his blade free he turned to see another animal charging at him. It had its head lowered and bounded forward on its massive forearms. He stood his ground and jumped at the moment of impact clutching the beast around the neck. Shocked by its new passenger the Volith skidded to a stop. Vas expertly slipped his forearm under the creature's chin and wrapped his legs around its back. Grabbing his forearm with his other hand he squeezed with all his considerable might. The creature tried to prize the parasite from its back, but the Emperor tucked his head in and continued to tighten his grip. The creature fell backwards. Its weight knocked the air from Vas's lungs but he did not release his choke. The Emperor's arms burnt with effort and finally the Volith slumped.

He tried to squeeze out from under the dead carcass but before he could get free the body of the Volith was tossed to one side. Vas breathed deeply, filling his lungs. He stared into the hungry reptile eyes that stood before him. The beast grabbed him by the arm and flung him violently across the clearing. He collided into a tree and slid to the floor. His vision swam and through the haze he saw the dribbling maw open and a fork tongue flick across its teeth, as the Volith closed on its prey.

The Emperor shut his eyes and succumbed to the darkness. His mind soared free and he felt himself floating. He looked down on his body. It seemed so small and insignificant. He heard a sound. A shout. It was his father, he was calling out to him. Anger boiled through his thoughts and at that instant he felt an inexorable pull back towards his mortal shell. He heard the shout again. This time he opened his eyes. In front of him stood Var, drenched in Volith blood.

"Come on you sons of the diseased" he yelled, completely lost in a kill frenzy.

A Volith bundled out from the jungle, and even though the mist was racing back the creature had only one thought. Var ran to meet it. As he closed he used the dead body of a slain animal and jumped into the air. He brought his knees up in a tuck position. The Volith tried to stop its charge but Var brought one of his blades down slicing the side of the creature's face off. He landed and spun his other sword cutting the Volith's leg in two beneath the knee. The animal fell as it tried to stand on its severed stump. A swipe across its stomach and another across its neck stilled the thrashing beast.

The trees ahead splintered and cracked and the sound of falling timber echoed towards the two men. The head of a giant Volith appeared through the undergrowth. It sniffed at the pile of its dead brothers. It threw back its head and roared beating its chest with its fists. Var had gone. The creature eyed the semi-conscious Emperor. As it stalked towards him he saw other smaller Volith arrive. They collected the bodies of their own kind and that of Dumonii and Magta and ran back into the dense jungle.

The solitary giant creature coughed saliva onto the floor as it started to breath clean air. The Emperor looked above its left shoulder and saw Var climbing out along a branch. His heavy artificial leg snagged and cracked a twig. The Volith's eyes flicked up. Var dived towards the animal. Before it could bring up its forearms Var landed on its back each blade burrowing deep into its flesh. Var pulled them free and repeatedly stabbed the creature. Green blood splashed up into his face as he continued to lacerate the animal's back. The animal fell into the ground as Var's crazed assault did not slow. Leaving one blade protruding from its back he walked around the prone creature and in several shuddering blows chopped through its neck.

Physically and mentally exhausted Var fell to his knees. The Emperor rubbed the back of his head and stood. He was unstable and he wobbled towards the ocean man. He placed his hand on his shoulder.

"Thank you my brother" he whispered. Var turned and stood. Tears had made tracks through the green blood covering his face. The Emperor looked into the eyes of his half-brother and didn't recognise the person who stared back. "Come. We must continue onwards. Our loss will be for nothing if we do not reach the city."

He watched as the Var he knew slowly returned to the killing machine he had become.

"Gero and Hanelore are out still out there. I will go no further until we have found them. When we return we will bury our dead" said Var.

The Emperor did not argue and followed the ocean man into the jungle. Shu was cresting the mountains and the insects and birds were beginning their morning chorus. Completely depleted of energy Var could hardly lift his sword to clear the vegetation from their path. They continued onwards until they saw the round basket of Hanelore's balloon hanging high up in the trees. Beneath it, on the churned forest floor sat Gero.

Var walked up to the cross-legged giant. He sheathed his swords and held out his open hand. Gero clasped it and stood. He embraced the ocean man. The Emperor hung his head in respect.

*

It was early afternoon by the time they had buried the bodies that the Volith had not stolen away. They marked each grave with a single stave. Of the four hundred souls that had left the old Dumonii city less than half remained. The relayed news that Hanelore had fallen just after they had taken off hit his sons hard. Gero had walked out into the desert to be alone. The Emperor and Lothair had organised the survivors. They were ready for the trek across the desert to the city of light.

Var knelt beside Bronsur's grave. He removed the small bone idol from around his neck. She had given it to him when they had first met. He draped it over the wooden stake.

"It was my privilege to have known you. You always brought out the best in me, and saw what others could not. You gave me strength when I could find none and gave me wisdom when my senses left me wanting. You were the best part of me. I will leave you now, but part of my heart will be with you always, and I will carry your essence in what remains of mine. Farewell and peace my love."

Chapter 10 - The Eternal Trial

The battered and forlorn survivors trudged across the desert plateau. Rocky islands interspersed between the soft dunes, made the walking easier. The wide barren expanse was a stark contrast against the lush green jungle. Despite the sweltering temperatures it was similar in a way to the icy landscape of Gebshu. Apart from the occasional lizard scurrying for cover it seemed devoid of life.

Undeterred by the harsh environment the small group continued onwards towards their goal. For perhaps the first time since they had left Asturia, their goal was clear. It was unavoidably clear. It would have been easy to mistake the city that lay ahead of them for one of the mountains or volcanoes, such was its size.

It rose from the hazy desert like a god-like guardian. Row upon row of levels decreasing in size as it towered up into the sky. From a distance these tiers had resembled a stepped pyramid but as they drew closer they could see each level incorporated grand buildings and what looked like gardens surrounded by outer walls. The light, which must have illuminated the entire desert at night, was still glowing. It was harder to make out, set against the bright sky. Even from this distance the gargantuan scale of the construction was apparent. Although the base wall was party obscured by dust clouds and heat haze, it was taller than the pyramid they had just left behind in the jungle. The smooth vertical stone reared up like some impossible cliff face.

Throughout the day they closed the distance and the colossal city started to fill their view. The weary travellers were transfixed by the mountain-city. Each step closer revealed a further detail. The greenery they had witnessed at a distance was indeed gardens. But even the scale of these was enormous. Tall, full grown trees, complete with resident flocks of birds circling above made up these natural havens in between the buildings. What also looked like the top of a waterfall cascaded down into the complex.

The rough desert floor and sand dunes underfoot gave way to smooth rock. It showed signs of mechanical intervention with tooling marks and bore holes criss-crossing its surface. The perfectly flat rock stretched out in either direction and looked to continue right up to the outer wall. Whatever natural formation had once stood here, it had long been cleared.

As they travelled across the levelled rock they saw a large opening in the ground. It had not been visible until they were almost on top of it. A wide track spiralled down into the bedrock making a cone like depression in the ground. There obviously had not been enough stone above the surface, so the creators of the great city had quarried into the earth for more material. This necklace of conical holes surrounded the entire complex.

What looked like some form of entrance scarred the otherwise flawless wall. The enormous barricade now blocked out their view of the rest of the city. As the afternoon turned to early evening the shadow from the city reached out to touch the edge of the forest. The slight drop in temperature from the shade was a welcome relief.

"What is the plan? Do we just walk up and knock on the door?" asked Gero.

"I hadn't really thought this far ahead" replied Var. "But that seems like as good an idea as any other."

The gate was similar in design and size to that which they had encountered at the Pillars of Itna. There were no other signs of an entrance or any other openings. Now at the foot of the wall it stretched up so high that the top was blurred. As Var stared up at the unique construction he started to feel dizzy. He shook his head and looked away.

"I feel it is safe to say that if they won't open the door, then we have no way of getting in" said Var.

"Well let us hope that somebody is home" replied Gero. Var looked back at the drained but expectant faces. If the door did not open then this would be the end of the line for most of them. The Doyen inspected the door. It was carved with scenes of battles and strange animals; some looked like the Volith. There was no handle, hatch or anything else that could be used to attract attention.

"Lothair do you think you could use your hammer to politely knock on the door?" suggested Var.

"Of course" replied the Titan stepping forward and removing the dire weapon from his back. He rested the hammer head on the floor and was about to heft it over his shoulder when a loud bang made them jump. The Emperor drew his sword.

"I know we should be prepared but perhaps we should wait until we know what lies behind the doors before we show any signs of aggression" said Var.

"That is a fair point" replied the Emperor sheathing his sword. The bang sounded once more before the grating of stone on stone and the meshing of gears signalled the opening of the doors. They slowly moved apart and as soon as the gap was wide enough Var stepped through. As before there was a series of doors. Each was sliding back into the walls, floor and ceiling. He walked through the arched tunnel which bore its way through the outer wall out into an open space. It was open to the sky but the light barely reached them as a short distance away was another huge wall identical to the one he had just walked through. It stretched out in all directions creating a deep gulley between it and the outer wall. There was however no sign of another gateway.

As the rest of the alliance crowded into the man-made gorge the outer doors began to close. As the last of them slammed shut, another loud rasping sound thundered out.

In front of them what looked like a single piece of stone that stretched the entire height of the wall, moved. It sent dust billowing into the air as the grinding noise echoed inside, and the mammoth pillar descended.

Var's heart pounded in his chest. He looked at the Emperor, embarrassed that he might hear it.

As the gigantic block moved downwards they could see another behind it moving upwards.

"I don't think they get too many visitors" said Gero.

"Not unwanted ones at least" said Var.

As the pillar neared the ground, Var and those around him moved warily backwards. On top of the now level slab was a machine identical to Solon. The only differences were that instead of a circular wheel on its left arm it sported another fist guard. The other striking difference was that it was in immaculate condition. Unlike the rusting, flaking guardian on Gebshu this machine looked as if it had just been constructed. The metal pistons and hydraulic rams glistened whilst the red and blue paintwork had a mirror like finish. The light at the centre of its head glowed a steady amber colour.

[State your purpose] blurted the machine.

Var stepped forward.

"We have travelled from the planet Gebshu. We wish to speak with the creators. We are creator born" offered Var. There was no reply at first. The machine emitted a sequence of bleeps and pings.

[Wait] replied the gleaming guardian.

The internal gears started to whirr once more and the pillar on which the machine stood started to rise up into the air.

"Good job we are not in any hurry" said Gero.

"Yes" replied Var. "And I am glad he didn't want proof we were creator born. That didn't go that well last time. At least there is someone here. That must be a good sign."

"Maybe the whole place is populated by machines. Perhaps our Dumonii ancestors have long since died out" suggested the Emperor.

"Well if it is just those things that live here we will be in for a short conversation" said Gero.

They waited for some time until the pillar started to move downwards again. As the guardian came into view they could see someone standing next to it. This time the pillar stopped just above them. An old man shuffled to the edge of the stone block. He was dressed simply in a red tunic that reached the floor. Another red scarf was wrapped around his head and across his face. He lifted his arm slowly and removed the material away revealing a short cropped white beard. His features were impossibly old.

Deep wrinkles filled his dark skinned visage. In his other hand he held a white staff decorated at its head with a jewelled scarab.

"My name is Var-Son-Gednu..." The Doyen halted mid sentence as the old man held up his hand indicating for him to stop.

"Your name is of no importance to me. It is best if this exchange is kept on a formal footing" said the old man. "You referred to yourselves as creator born. That language can only have come from the Pillar Guardian. Therefore at least some of you must have satisfied his programming. This means that you are indeed descendants. But is obvious even to my old eyes that some of you are not." He looked directly at Gero and Lothair. "You are Magta are you not?" he asked.

"We are" replied Lothair. "We and the few brothers and sisters you see before you are the last of our kind."

"Interesting" replied the old man. "I would have thought your kind would have long since left the world of the living."

"Well we've come close a few times, but we are still breathing old man" growled Gero.

"We mean no harm" interrupted Var."Our journey here has not been the easiest and we have suffered much along the way. Please forgive our fatigued state."

"Indeed. Why have you come to the city of Aspect?" questioned the old man.

"Our planet is dying. We set out in search of the Gods. We hoped they would listen to our plea and reverse the situation. When we reached the Pillars of Itna and spoke with the Guardian Solon, we realised that we were following in the footsteps of our ancient forefathers. We had hoped to meet you, the creators and perhaps you would have answers" explained Var.

The old man chuckled to himself.

"Ah the naivety of the young races. I do not know of any 'creators'. I can only assume this is an idiosyncrasy of Solon's antiquated program. We are collectively known as the Eternals and I am Faro. I am a representative of the All Fathers. As for Gods. It has been a while since I heard that phrase. I have read that it was a common belief, that all powerful beings were the masters of all life and the universe, but that is nonsense. Only a fool would believe in such stories."

Faro stroked his beard.

"You have endured much and it shows great resolve that you have made it to our gates. No doubt you met the very unpleasant Volith in the ironically named New Sagen. It seems as if some of you bear the scars of their attention. Even so, I cannot simply open the doors and welcome you into our home. "

"We cannot go back. What would you have us do?" pleaded Var.

"Only those deemed worthy may enter our hallowed city. Two of you must be tested. They must enter the trials. If they are successful we will grant you access and the All Fathers will answer your questions" replied Faro.

"And what if we are unsuccessful?" asked the Emperor.

"There is no second chance in the trials. It is success or death. For the rest - You will have to take your chances in the desert or return to the jungle." replied the old man.

"If we should prove worthy, will you grant entry to all of us?"

The old man stroked his beard as he thought about the question.

"The All Fathers will have to decide upon the fate of the Magta, but the rest of you, yes, you will be welcomed" said Faro.

"That doesn't sound like much of deal" grumbled Gero.

"I believe our options are limited" said Lothair. "Var, I would be happy to undergo the trials."

The old man tapped his staff against the stone.

"The Magta may not compete" he said abruptly.

"Then I will take the trials" said Var defiantly. The Emperor stepped forward to stand by the shoulder of the Doyen.

"I will join my brother."

"So be it." Faro tapped his staff once again and the guardian machine behind him beeped and clicked. The stone pillar started to rise and at the same time the area which contained Var and the Alliance started to sink. Dust swirled up into the air as the huge platform descended. They could see large grooves in the walls upon which the platform rolled. It continued into the ground and then jolted to a stop. To one end of the platform was a small doorway.

"I don't like this" said Gero grabbing Var's arm.

"As Lothair has mentioned we don't have much choice my friend. We are so close now. The answers to all our questions lie inside. A safe haven for our people and an end to our suffering. We will argue the case of the Magta if we survive. Rest assured I will not abandon you and your people" said Var.

"I am not concerned for myself, you know that. The fate of our race has been on borrowed time for many seasons. What happens to us has already been decided, but I would see you fulfil your destiny even if it takes my last breath"

"Let us hope it does not come to that" said Var smiling. He clasped forearms with the giant before finally Gero pulled him close and patted him on the back.

"Good luck my friend" said the giant.

Var and the Emperor walked into the dark entrance and no sooner had they entered a stone door slammed shut and the platform started to rise obscuring the door way.

*

As the pair walked into the tunnel lights flickered to life all along the walls. Var followed the Emperor as they came out into a large cavern. Halfway across was a massive metal cube. It was suspended by chains and cogs above a deep chasm. There were steps up to a small door on the side of the cube. Var approached the edge with caution and lent forward. The heat from below caused him to pull back suddenly. He shielded his face and looked again. Far below, at the bottom of the divide bubbled molten rock. The two men looked up as they heard a familiar tapping sound.

Across on the other side stood Faro.

"This is the first of three trials. It is the trial of confusion. You must enter the cube and make it through to the other side" explained the old man.

"And what awaits us on the inside?" asked the Emperor.

"There is nothing inside to harm you. It is simply a three dimensional maze. Find the route through and you will have conquered this trial" said Faro.

"That sounds simple" said Var.

"However" started Faro. "It has a further level of complexity. I will start this timer. When it ends the cube will rotate around one axis. It will do this another five times. If you have not made it to the other side after the final turn the supports holding the cube will release it into the lava chamber below."

"I take it back" said Var. "This is far from simple. Do you have any ideas on how we should tackle this?"

"None" replied the Emperor. Var looked around the floor and picked up a small stone.

"We are ready" he called out.

The Emperor sprinted up the steps and into the device.

"Shall we split up or stick together?" he asked.

"I will follow you" said Var ducking into the small entrance.

Inside it was dimly lit with lights similar to those they had passed in the tunnel. They were set behind glass in the metal walls. At the end of where they had entered was a further metal wall. As they reached it they had the choice of going left or right.

"I will mark each turn we take and each square we cross" said Var. "That way we can trace our steps back."

They turned left and crawled along the narrow space. As they reached the end the way was blocked.

"Above you" said Var.

The Emperor stood up and climbed upwards. He reached back and helped Var up the narrow gap. As they started to make their way along the next crawlspace the metal creaked. The whole cube then tipped one hundred and eighty degrees sending the two men flying into the walls. It stopped. They were now on the roof of the space they had just crawled along.

"I know why this is called the trial of confusion" said Var.

"Quickly" said the Emperor as he scampered down the passageway. They made it three more corners and a further vertical before the cube turned again. The Emperor fell backwards on top of Var.

"It was a dead end. We must retrace our steps back to the beginning" shouted the Emperor. Var turned and following the marks he had scratched into the metal plates as he scurried along through the tunnels. By the time they had made it back to the start it had turned over once more. It was rotating around a different axis each time and without the markings they would have become completely disorientated. Var made way and the Emperor squeezed by him. They made it some distance into the device, randomly deciding a direction when then came to a divergence, and bracing themselves against the walls as the cube turned over.

They reached another dead end. The Emperor cursed and the machine turned once again.

"We are running out of time. How many is that?" he asked.

"That's five" replied Var.

They hurried back along following Var's scratchings in the metal. They came to a three way intersection.

"Which way?" asked the Emperor.

"Left" said Var. "No wait!" he yelled. He looked down the other route they had not yet explored. He could see a faint yellow light flickering against the glass.

"That way" he pointed. The Emperor scrambled past and Var hurried after him. They rounded the corner and could see light from the exit ahead.

"We're nearly there. Hurry!" shouted the Emperor. He shot forward. The cube rotated for the final time. Var thumped into the metal sides. Before he could regain his senses a firm hand gripped him and dragged him forwards. The Emperor unceremoniously bundled Var out of the door and dived out behind him. Var wheezed as the Emperor's knee landed on his stomach. There were loud clangs and the two men looked back to see the metal box disappear into the chasm. Var crawled to the edge and looked over. The cube bobbed in the lava before vanishing beneath its glowing surface. Ahead of them a door opened.

As they walked into the second chamber they saw the red robed figure of Faro appear from a balcony set high up on the opposite wall. In the centre of the chamber was a tall column. Spiralling around it were metal pegs. They continued to twist around the pillar all the way to the top. The pillar stood about nine times the height of the Emperor. The chamber roof had been carved into a conical shape to allow for this strange monolith. On the far side of the pillar was another door.

"Well done. I am glad to see you have made it past the first trial" said Faro. "This is the second. This is called the trial of choice" explained the old man.

"How many people have even got through the first part?" asked Var.

"You are the first" replied Faro. "The trial of choice as its name indicates will present you both will some interesting decisions. One of you must climb to the top of the pillar. At its summit there is a button. This will open the door you can see opposite. Once opened you have a small amount of time to climb back down and make it through. The weight of the door will increase with every passing moment. So you must decide who climbs and who will hold the door. If the weight becomes too great you may choose to enter the doorway and leave your friend behind, or indeed you may choose to remain in the chamber also. Once the door closes the room will fill with water. There is one last thing. If you cannot open the door before the ball reaches the floor. It will remain locked and you will both drown. Make your choice."

A stone ball dropped from high in the ceiling and started to roll around the cone in a previously unnoticed channel.

"I am stronger than you, I should hold the door" said the Emperor.

"You are" conceded Var. "But there is no way I can climb that pillar quickly. The rungs get further apart as they ascend. Even if I could get to the top I would never make it down in time."

"That is true. Hold the door for as long as you can. If I am not back go through on your own. For the sake of both our peoples we cannot fail." The Emperor did not give Var a chance to argue and leapt onto the first rung. Var moved to the doorway as he watched the Emperor climb the pillar.

As the ocean man had described, the rungs were getting further apart. They were also getting shorter. Vas realised with horror that the posts on which he was standing were slowly retracting into the column. He continued to climb opting to miss out every other post. He neared the top and leapt for the last rung. His hands clasped around it. He had to move his inner hand as the moving post threatened to pinch his skin. He reached up grabbing the rim of the pillar. He hauled himself over the edge and stretched out thumping the stone button at the centre.

"It's open!" he heard Var call out. He lowered himself down. The posts could now only just accommodate both his feet at the same time. He made his way downwards as fast as he could.

As the stone door opened Var moved beneath it. As soon as it had reached the top it started to drop. He reached up and held the door with his arms. He strained, but the stone was too heavy. He allowed it to fall further and then wedged himself under it so the stone landed on his shoulder. He held the weight. The pressure on his shoulder started to rapidly increase as if stone upon stone was being piled on top.

"Hurry!" yelled Var. Straining to catch a glimpse of the Emperor. Pain flared in his shoulder and he knew he would buckle within moments. He bent forwards and the door lowered further onto his back. He reached down and unbuckled his artificial leg. Holding the door on his back for another few moments he fell to the floor. The door started to lower and Var rammed the wooden limb against the wall. The door jammed on the obstruction. Var crept under the door and looked back. The leg started to creak and he could hear the wood starting to fracture.

He saw two feet land and the Emperor roll onto his shoulder. He dived for the door. Var grabbed his arms and dragged him through. The leg splintered and the door crashed further down. The increased weight of the door slowly pulverised the artificial limb until the door was completely sealed.

The two men lay breathing heavily on the floor.

"It can't get any harder than that, can it?" said the Emperor rolling to his knees.

"Well I hope it's not a race, otherwise this is as far as I go" panted Var. The Emperor helped him to his feet and supported him as Var hopped along the connecting tunnel.

It opened out into a large circular room. On the far side was a huge door and set up into the rock on the right hand side was what looked like a viewing gallery. A red robed figure was standing within it.

"Congratulations" applauded Faro. "That was most impressive. I can see how you were able to make it to our gates. I am impressed by your resourcefulness."

"You can save the praise for when we have completed the final task" stated the Emperor.

"As you wish" replied Faro. "This is the third, and as you correctly identified, the final task. It is the trial of combat. Our civilisations have grown strong on the back of our ability to wage war. The prowess of a warrior in battle has long been a revered trait above all others. As we have grown as a race I will admit we have found other ways, and violence is not now our preferred method of negotiation. However a citizen of Aspect must be able to demonstrate that most base trait if so required. The rules are simple. Defeat your opponent and you win. We will then open the gates to you and your people."

"I wish I had my hammers" muttered the Emperor.

"Here" said Var. "Take these." He handed over his two curved swords. "They were crafted by the Magta. The edge never dulls and will cut through almost anything. They are better off in your hands as my contribution to this final trial is going to be limited."

"Thank you brother" said the Emperor. He gave Var his wide bladed sword and the ocean man used it as a makeshift crutch. The two men made their way into the centre of the ring. The door on the other side opened. They could make out a red light. In a blur the mechanical guardian that had greeted them at the city gates stomped into the arena.

"This is Saladin" announced Faro. "He is all that stands between you and the end of your journey."

"No. That's not fair" said Var. "We couldn't stop the last one, we couldn't even dent it."

"We will find a way" said the Emperor, and he ran headlong at the machine.

He ducked beneath the first fist and rolled under the second. The guardian was in offensive mode, and its armour plating had rolled down covering the front. Both knuckledusters were also in place over its mechanical hands. The Emperor ran between its legs slicing at the hydraulic rams on both sides. Even the razor sharp Magta blades had little impact. They sparked off the metal leaving shallow scratches in their wake.

The machine started to circle. If it had a weakness this was it. Its speed in turning was slow. If the Emperor could keep on the move and keep Saladin chasing him they might be able to find an opening. As the machine clanked around Var made his way towards its back. Hopping as best he could he positioned himself in behind its right leg. Besides the pistons and rams there were several metal pipes that curled around the ankle joint. Balancing himself he raised his sword and sliced it down onto the small pipe. Hot steam hissed out from a tiny crack. Supporting himself with one hand on the guardian's shin armour he thrust the sword downwards once more. This time the point sliced through the lower pipe. Oil pumped through the severed pipe and started to spill over Saladin's foot.

Without warning the guardian's arm flew backwards. It caught Var on the shoulder and span him away. He fell on the dusty floor and Saladin turned on the struggling warrior. Sensing Var's situation the Emperor climbed on the machine's back. He repeatedly hacked at the armour . The swords succeeded in denting the plating but nothing more. Var ducked beneath a fist before using the sword to help himself stand. The hand came swinging back. Var jumped to the side but Saladin grabbed his sword. The pistons in its hands wheezed and closed shattering the blade. Before he could move the massive armoured fist thumped Var high in to the air. He landed in a heap some distance from the machine.

Saladin now turned his attention to the Emperor. Vas ducked and dodged as the metal hands tried to claw him from his position on its back. The Emperor could see that despite his efforts he was making no impact on the machine. He slid down onto the ground and looked out to where Var lay. He clanged his swords against Saladin's armour as he moved away from the guardian trying to give himself some space. As he moved, Saladin's hand closed over his shoulder. He dropped to one knee just as the metal fingers hissed and closed ripping his shoulder plate away. The straps burnt his flesh as they were torn away but he avoided serious injury.

Running to the far side of the chamber the Emperor unclasped his chest plate and the remaining pauldron. He threw the armour onto the ground. His torso glistened with sweat outlining his muscles that were pumping with adrenaline. He would have been a match for any living warrior or beast, but Saladin was not alive. It was simply following its program to destroy.

As the giant machine came towards him he noticed the dark liquid running onto its foot. Var had injured it. With a spark of hope he ducked beneath the oncoming fist and jumped onto its foot. He launched himself up and over the guardian's shin guard just as the other fist came smashing in. Vas avoided the blow and the impact from Saladin's own fist cracked its leg armour. The Emperor looked down to see oil still squirting from the broken pipe. He lashed down, opened the tear further.

The machine lifted its foot and stamped down. The shock sent the Emperor sprawling onto the floor. As he recovered the armoured fist slammed into him. The blow sent him skittering across the ground and he felt a searing pain all down his left side. Struggling to stand he could not avoid the follow up strike. The spiked knuckle protector of Saladin lifting him into the air and depositing him in front of the large doorway. The jagged metal fist had opened up a deep wound across his stomach and chest. The Emperor coughed, spitting blood onto the floor. He dropped his swords and tried to stem the blood loss with his hands.

The shadow of the God machine loomed over him.

"Stand down!" came the shout from across the cavern. During the battle Var had used every last fibre of his strength and had climbed to the balcony. He now held Faro in his grip with the top of his knife drawing blood at the old man's throat.

"Tell that infernal machine to stand down, or I will

cut your throat" warned Var.

"Terminate exercise!" shouted Faro.

The huge machine stopped immediately. Its defensive armour rolled back over its head and its fist guards rotated. It moved past the stricken Emperor and through the opening doors. Var spun the old man.

"Well done young Var" congratulated Faro. "The test of combat is a difficult one. Not all fights can be won by brute force. There is always another way to defeat a superior opponent, and you have succeeded in finding Saladin's only weakness - myself."

"Does this mean we have completed the trials?" asked Var.

"It does."

"And what about Vas, my people and the Magta" he continued.

"Well I suggest we get your brother some medical attention. Your people will be granted access to the city. The All Fathers have yet to decide on the race of giants, but they will be welcomed in the meantime. Come, I am sure you are in need of rest. When you have recovered I will show you the wonders of Aspect.

Chapter 11 - Into the Ether

They spent three rotations recovering in the palatial surroundings of the city. They had attended as promised to the wounds of the Emperor and to Var. The two men sat on a garden terrace looking out over the colossal construction. Birds sang and flew from tree to tree and insects buzzed around the plethora of flowers and fragrant bushes. Water flowed in a manmade stream along the edge of the gardens; part of a complicated irrigation system not too dissimilar to the food ziggurats back on Son-Gebshu, but on a much grander scale.

"How is the wound?" asked Var.

"Surprisingly good. It feels tight, but that would have been fatal back on the moon. Their medical skills are impressive. How about you? The new leg seems to be a good fit" replied the Emperor.

"It is a marvel. I thought the one Hanelore constructed was amazing but this is a whole other class. It is so much lighter and it responds to the muscle movements in my leg. I think it is actually better than my real leg."

"Excuse me. I hope I am not interrupting" said Faro as he appeared from within the glass house at the rear of the terrace. "I thought I would find you here. This is one of the most stunning views of the city and the mountains beyond is it not?"

"It is" replied the Emperor.

"Have you made a decision?" asked Var.

"Straight to the point I see. Yes the All Fathers have decided to let the Magta stay. There are so few left that it will not be long before their kind is lost to legend" explained Faro.

"Still no room for emotion I see. How is it that your people survive? There don't seem to be that many of you either" retorted Var.

"Emotion can cloud judgement. I have no malice towards your friends Var. They would be the first to agree with my summation. As for the Eternals, well the key is in our name. I promised you answers, and that is what I am here for. Where would you like me to start?" asked Faro.

"The Gods" said Var. "Why do they not exist? Why can't we save the planet?"

"Ah yes, the relentless search for something greater than ourselves. I cannot say definitively that there are no Gods, but in our study of the universe the argument for all powerful immortal beings controlling the worlds and those upon them has no substance. When you look up at the night sky you can see millions of stars. There are millions more that you cannot see. Shu is just one of these stars. It, like everything else has a lifespan. We cannot comprehend the near infinite timescale of this lifespan, but it does have a beginning and an end. It is simply unfortunate that you and your people find yourselves living in the time of its death."

"But if it is going to die, then why did your ancestors move here? This world will also die eventually according to that theory" asked Var.

"Indeed. You are correct. At the time of the last great cataclysm that issue was still up for debate. There were those who believed the exodus to the moon of Son-Gebshu would provide enough time for our ancestors to find a solution. There were others who believed only a move to another planet in our system could provide the time required. That is why the All Fathers constructed the celestial gate and travelled here to the planet of Arcshu. As you have correctly ascertained this planet will one day follow the decay of Gebshu and its moon. That time is far in the distance and cannot be measured in our lifetimes."

"So what happened when the All Fathers arrived here? " asked the Emperor.

"Yes, I forget you have visited the inappropriately named New Sagen. As you are by now aware the core of this planet is extremely volatile. The sulphurous gas is just one way in which it materialises. When we arrived, the location within the jungle with access to food and water resources seemed like a good place to settle. We encountered the Volith during those early days and built the defences that now crumble into the jungle."

"How did you manage that? We were there for

only a few rotations and they halved our numbers" said Var.

"Our technology is and was further advanced than you can imagine. The guardian machines are just one example of this. Beneath our feet lie hundreds of such machines that were used to build New Sagen and this great city. We did not build either by hand." Faro laughed.

"As we set our minds to the study of the universe we acknowledged we required a more substantial home, and hence the city of Aspect was conceived."

"That still does not explain how you have survived this long. As you say the Magta will eventually die out because of their numbers. Even if there were thousands of you I do not understand how you are still alive" queried Var.

"Once again your intuition serves you well. There were thousands of us. Many thousands. But as you say we would have become extinct long ago. How can I explain this?" Faro stroked his white beard.

"The trees and plants that you see all about you. Most, if not all of these are now extinct. We brought the seeds of every plant here from Gebshu and now we are able to grow them once more. We can also mix the seeds to grow variations and cultivate new species. It is the same with us. We have a library of genetic information. Every five revolutions one hundred brothers and one hundred sisters are born in our laboratories. When my time of passing and that of my siblings arrives there will be another generation to take our place. This is how it has always been and will continue to be so."

"That doesn't sound like much of a life" commented Var.

"What happened to all the others that came here, are they dead?" asked the Emperor.

"Some maybe. But most take the next step along the pathway of knowledge" replied Faro.

"What does that mean?" asked Var.

"I think it is perhaps time I showed you. Please follow me" instructed the old man.

The two men followed Faro into the heart of the building. Var kept flexing forward on his artificial toes as they walked.

"You'll wear it out" smiled Vas.

They arrived at an arched wooden doorway. Carved into the many layers of the architrave were hundreds of words and symbols. Some Var could recognise, others were obscure and looked more like pictograms than words. As they followed the old man into the room they stared upwards. It was a vast circular room with a domed ceiling. It had six levels. On every one the walls were stocked with thousands of books.

"This is the library. You asked about our lives. We have long since transcended the base needs such as wealth and power. It is knowledge that consumes us. This library is one of thirty four that exist throughout the city. Each is dedicated to a specific study. This one contains everything we have learned about the universe. Come there is something else I would show you."

They followed Faro through a door on the far side. It was another enormous room although not as high. Taking up the majority of the space was the strangest contraption Var had ever seen. Thousands upon thousands of small spheres all connected by thin metal rods. At the centre of each group of spheres were numerous cogs and gears. Var and Vas were ignoring the machine staring instead at the guardian that occupied an alcove at one end of the room.

"Ah yes, that is Semafore. He is unique amongst the guardian machines as you can probably see" explained Faro.

Semafore was identical to Saladin apart from having no metal armature. All of the leg, arm and body armour had been replaced with a marbled white stone.

"What is this?" asked Var pointing to the collection of metal globes on the central machine. The old man walked to the side of the room and pulled on a lever. The machine whirred into life. Whole sections started to rotate, tilt and spin. Then small groups of spheres within each section began to spin and move. Several of them glowed, some with a bright blue light and some yellow.

"This machine is a star map" explained Faro. "Each of the yellow orbs represents a star. Each of the blue orbs represents a planet. Each of these planets has the ability to support life."

"There are hundreds" exclaimed Var.

"Yes. And these are the ones we have found to date. We find more with every passing revolution. So now you know where the rest of your ancestors have gone" said Faro.

"They have travelled to these other worlds" said the Emperor.

"They are the pioneers of the universe" replied Faro.

"How?" said Var.

"I assume it was the light at the top of the city that first came to your attention. You are familiar with the shimmer portals as you travelled here using one. The gateway at the top of the pyramid is our greatest achievement. It is called the Ether gate. From it we are able to travel across the vast expanse of space. Semafore acts as a scouting party. His unique construction enables him to travel to the planet we select. He collects samples before activating his armour. The stone surrounding him is the same as in the Ether Gate, and allows him to return to us. Although his time in the portal is limited, we have been able to ascertain the suitability of a planet for habitation."

"Why haven't you left? If this planet will eventually die why don't you leave?" asked Var.

"Oh we will. There is still so much to learn, but when the time comes, we will relocate."

"That is a lot to understand" smiled Var.

"That it is. I have explained it to you, because you must decide what your future holds. You are welcome to live out your time in our city. You will want for nothing here, and there is so much you still have to learn. Or, you can follow your forefathers and travel." Faro held up his arms and indicated to the revolving machine.

Var reached out and touched one of the glowing blue orbs. The machine stopped and the globe that he had indicated moved to the centre of the machine.

"A good choice. Its atmosphere is a mix of oxygen, nitrogen and argon quite suitable for your metabolism" explained Faro.

Var stared at the Emperor.

"I'll pack my things" smiled Vas.

*

Var, Vas and Lin made their way up the spiral staircase and out into the Ether Gate. The pillars of stone were like giant claws arching up over their heads. The black night sky hung behind the bright glow of the vibrating stones. Faro walked towards the group and handed Var a large tome.

"This book is called the 'Tale of Worlds'. It contains information on science, biology, engineering and most other subjects you may need to know. Keep it safe. It may save your lives. At the very least it will make your lives easier. I wish you well on your voyage."

"Not leaving without me are you?" came the gruff voice from behind the old man.

"We were wondering where you had got to. Did you forget something?" asked Var.

"Just a couple of things" smiled Gero.

"Food I'll wager" said Vas quietly.

"Don't you start. Look, if we are going to be adventuring together then let's get one thing straight you tiny bag of bones. I like my own space. I snore. I don't like mornings, and nobody but nobody touches my food. That applies to all of you" warned Gero.

"Can we leave him here?" whispered Lin.

"We need someone to carry the gear" replied Var.

The four companions stood at the centre of the gate as the frequency increased. The pitch grew and grew before silence enveloped them as the shimmer portal went ultra sonic.

"One last thing" asked Var. "Where are we going?"

"We have named the planet - Terra" replied Faro.

Epilogue

The ocean planet Gebshu quickly became the ice planet Gebshu. Over the next couple of seasons the increase in temperature in the summer months was not sufficient to melt the ice sheets. Life continued for a short while above and below but within only eight seasons the last of the Kekken sank to the depths. Those who had remained in Asturia battled out an existence in the harsh environment but even they succumbed to the bitter cold after only a few more seasons. Twenty seasons after the last exodus and all life had frozen. Darkness gripped the once vibrant world.

The moon of Son-Gebshu saw a minor rebirth under the watchful gaze of Tol-Son-Ray. He galvanised the remaining population and ruled for thirty-two revolutions. He died as predicted, an old man clutching to the arms of his precious throne. Dispute and quarrels between prospective heirs quickly undid his work and the moon suffered the full brunt of the climatic changes. Seven revolutions later the moon of Son-Gebshu also embraced the darkness.

The All Fathers and the descendants of the Dumonii, the Ocean Tribes and the Magta still look out from the city of Aspect at the heavens, absorbing and cataloguing each and every star and planet. On one of those tiny specks Var and his companions forge a new life.

That however is another story.

Island of Hope
THE SEA OF SERENITY

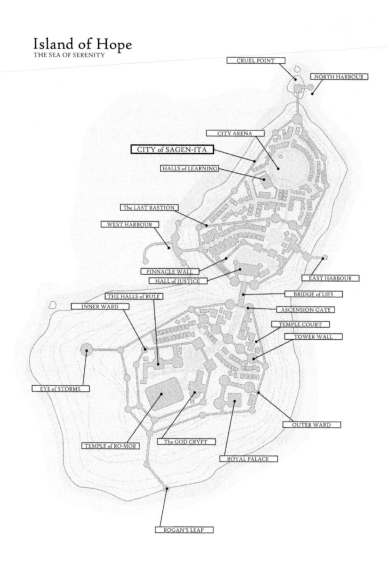

CRUEL POINT

NORTH HARBOUR

CITY ARENA

CITY of SAGEN-ITA

HALLS of LEARNING

The LAST BASTION

WEST HARBOUR

PINNACLE WALL

HALL of JUSTICE

EAST HARBOUR

THE HALLS of RULE

BRIDGE of LIES

INNER WARD

ASCENSION GATE

TEMPLE COURT

TOWER WALL

EYE of STORMS

OUTER WARD

TEMPLE of RO-MOR

The GOD CRYPT

ROYAL PALACE

ROGAN'S LEAP

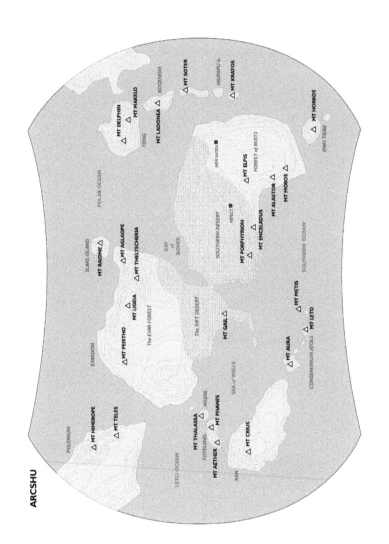

ARCSHU